MURDER IN NEW ORLEANS

By the same author:

Murder at Machu Picchu

Murder in Barbados

Murder in San Francisco

MURDER IN NEW ORLEANS

Mariann Tadmor

Copyright © 2007 by Mariann Tadmor.

ISBN:	Hardcover	978-1-4257-5582-9
	Softcover	978-1-4257-5580-5

All rights reserved. No part of this book may be reproduced or transmitted in any form or by any means, electronic or mechanical, including photocopying, recording, or by any information storage and retrieval system, without permission in writing from the copyright owner.

This is a work of fiction. Names, characters, places and incidents either are the product of the author's imagination or are used fictitiously, and any resemblance to any actual persons, living or dead, events, or locales is entirely coincidental.

This book was printed in the United States of America.

To order additional copies of this book, contact:
Xlibris Corporation
1-888-795-4274
www.Xlibris.com
Orders@Xlibris.com

38430

For
Ethan and Zackary
Joshua, Benjamin and Maia Ella
and Mika and Noah

Acknowledgments

My sincere thanks go to friends, to family, and to all faithful readers whose encouragement I value greatly. Not least, my appreciation goes to those supportive, energetic *SWEA* women whose activities in the New England Chapter (book club members, you know who you are), and in New Orleans, in particular, continue to inspire me. And, as always, I am indebted to Yoav Tadmor for his invaluable comments during the writing of this book.

Chapter 1

New Orleans, August 8, 2005

One came at me from the right, the other from the left.

I stopped a fraction of a second too long. Two against one were never my favorite odds and all I could do was concentrate on one at a time. I took three steps back to get my bearings. Couldn't find any.

If I'd had my .38 I could have taken a shot at them. As it was, what I had was Tae Kwon Do. I took another couple of steps back to prepare my stance.

They were both breathing noisily which marked them as possible martial arts practitioners. Or maybe just thugs with adenoids. It was a dark night.

The one on my left felt like my best bet. His shadow was square and compact. A solid target. Unfortunately, it was moving. I backed up some more. He stopped.

I took a deep breath and squared my shoulders. I bent both knees, stepped up with my left foot, lifted my right knee and aimed my jumping front kick high to his chest. It landed perfectly.

"Ouuuw," he said and went down.

I spun around and lost my sense of direction. The second guy moved in and I barreled up against him. He took one step back and I rammed my head into his solar plexus. His middle was hard as a rock.

He locked his arms around me, no martial arts technique here. He let go of me abruptly, held me at arms length with his left hand and popped me in the nose with his right.

Blood gushed from both nostrils but I was too stunned to cry out. He turned me around, grabbed my hair and dragged me along on my butt. My arms flailed but got a hold of nothing. He tossed me against a wall and kept a grip on my hair. My ears were ringing.

He bent down and belched beer breath in my face.

"Pretty girl like you. Go home and stop looking for Ricky Wilson. Next time you won't be this lucky."

He let go of me and I skidded to the ground. Usually people call me girl at their peril but I was too pre-occupied with my nose to lecture him.

They took their time leaving. As if I was no threat at all. Which happened to be very true at the moment.

I wanted to shout 'Who's Ricky Wilson,' but it seemed I'd developed lockjaw.

I pinched the bridge of my nose to stop the bleeding, bent my head back and rested it against the wall. Maybe I passed out briefly. I couldn't tell. I felt woozy and out of it.

I moved arms and legs tentatively. Stiff but not broken. I turned around on my knees, held on to the wall, and slowly got to my feet. Blood still trickled down my chin and I smeared it around with my sleeve. Then I slid down the wall again and sat some more. I had my wallet in one pants pocket and found tissue in the other. I stuck two pieces in my nostrils and was ready to go.

The street was as quiet as before the attack and if anyone had heard or seen anything they had no intention of investigating. Must be all in a night's work. A light went on in one upper-story window and was turned off just as fast. Someone walked out of a door further down the street and disappeared at a trot.

I re-traced my previous steps slowly, back down to St. Ann. I passed St. Louis Cathedral with its white facade and three black pointed spires, went directly across to the elegant wrought-iron fence and into Jackson Square. I by-passed necking couples on wooden benches and went through the center of the park. Andrew Jackson's horse teetered on its two hind legs and pigeons rested cozily on his head. For the second time that day, I passed the 1850 Antebellum House, and ignored several gift and candy shops on the square.

A few more steps and I was at Bob Makowski's borrowed townhouse in the Pontalba Apartments.

I pounded violently on his front door.

Chapter 2

"Who's Ricky Wilson?" I said.

Bob Makowski stared at my bloodied face. I sniffled and my nose started bleeding again.

"Jamie Prescott. Chrissake," he said.

"Who's Ricky Wilson," I repeated.

"Chum from the FBI."

"Figured it had something to do with you," I said. "Two gorillas beat me up and told me to stay away from Ricky Wilson," I said and touched my swollen cheek. "What's he done?"

"He's disappeared."

"Must've stepped on someone's toes," I said.

"Came down here to retire," Bob said.

"When?"

"Six months ago."

"To do what?" I said.

"To play the drums at a jazz club in the French Quarter."

"From special agent to drummer?"

"Someone at the Bureau swore to it," Bob said.

"And why not. Sounds like someone's dream come true."

"Came over him very suddenly."

"Never mentioned it?"

"Not to me he didn't."

"Show me his picture," I said.

Bob fished it out of his inside pocket.

Ricky Wilson was the kind of clean-cut, crewcut, spit-and-polish guy whom no witness would remember nor ever recognize. A very FBI kind of face.

"Any distinguishing marks?" I asked.

"None."

"No freckles or bad breath?"

Bob Makowski glared.

"Moving right along," I said.

I had winged it into New Orleans from Washington less than three hours ago—not knowing why Bob had summoned me but responding immediately to an urgent message—had checked into the Monteleone, and walked down to the address Bob had given me at the Pontalba Apartments on Jackson Square.

To my surprise he wasn't there so I'd left a note on the door. I'd sauntered down some side streets towards the French Quarter ignoring my own time-honored advice for tourists in New Orleans: don't walk around alone after dark.

"They must have followed me from here," I said. "Does that happen to all your visitors?"

"You're my first visitor."

"Where were you?"

"Out for a beer," Bob said.

"Without your cell phone?"

"Without. Sorry. Don't know how that happened."

"And vigilance used to be my middle name," I said.

"I bet you gave as good as you got," Bob said.

"Hardly." I touched my sore cheek.

"Sorry," Bob said again.

"Get me a Kleenex," I said. "Where's the bathroom?"

"Upstairs, next to the bedrooms."

"I'll be right back. Have any coffee?"

The sight in the mirror was not a feast for sore eyes. My left cheek was ballooning and taking on several hues of blue and red—which I pictured mutating into greens and yellows within a couple of days. My nose looked out of joint and continued to drip. I found some cotton and plugged up both nostrils but it was soon wet through.

"Got some ice-cubes?" I yelled down the stairs and heard a muffled reply. A moment later Bob came pounding up and handed me some cubes in a kitchen towel.

"Coffee's ready," he said. "Come down when you're fit to be seen in company."

The coffee was strong and bitter and it did the trick. I kept the ice on the bridge of my nose and soon the oozing stopped. Now my head started pounding.

"Got some pain-killer?"

Bob opened his fist and rolled a couple of Tylenol into my hand. I drank them down with coffee, leaned my head against the back of the sofa, and suddenly dozed off.

Bob shook me awake.

"That's long enough," he said. "Five minutes. Could be you have a concussion. Maybe we should find the emergency room?"

"No need to fuss." I covered my cheek with the ice-bag and kept it there off and on for the next fifteen minutes. I wanted to stay awake so I went from the comfortable sofa to a straight uncomfortable chair.

"You should give up travel agenting. You're much better at detecting," Bob said.

I threw in my gun a couple of years ago to become the owner of a travel agency in Bethesda. But Bob ignores my alternative life and keeps tossing hard-to-resist cases my way. Not to say that I don't run into a few sticky situations on my own. My problems, of course, are not all of a criminal investigative nature. I also keep dating the wrong men.

"It's no fun without you," Bob said.

Bob Makowski is a former FBI agent with a successful detective agency in Washington, D.C. He has no known skills in the martial arts or in any other kind of exercise. He can best be described as a couch potato.

“Those were ten good years,” Bob said. “And you were so young when I found you.”

“I was twenty-eight, and you didn’t find *me*, *I* found *you*.”

“True. Fresh out of college at the ripe old age of twenty-eight,” Bob said.

“That wasn’t college. That was grad school at GW. I got a late start because I married Roger in Paris and it took me a while to divorce him and return home.”

“Good thing you did.”

“My master’s in criminology was essential. Where would I’ve been without it?”

“That was theory, Jamie Prescott,” Bob said. “But who trained you to become a hot-shot private investigator?”

“You did.”

Okay, it’s true. I’m reputed to be a hot-shot female private investigator. I’m 42, unattached, half an inch short of six feet, and training for my black belt in Tae Kwon Do.

“Too bad you left me,” Bob said.

“I didn’t leave you. I’m here, aren’t I?”

The room we were sitting in on the second floor of the townhouse had been renovated in its original style from the 1800s.

“You know who built these row houses, of course,” I said.

“No, I don’t. I know who renovated this particular one, though.”

“Your rich friends in Washington?”

“Not that rich but they spend their winters here.”

“You must have noticed the initials A and P in the cast-iron balcony right outside these windows?”

“Nah, you know me, not one for artistic detail.”

“Stands for Almonester Pontalba. She was a baroness born in New Orleans.”

“Didn’t know we had royalty.”

“Her father was Spanish.”

“That would do it.”

“She married and lived in Paris, dueled with her father-in-law when he wanted her to sign over her estate. He shot off two of her fingers. She left her husband, returned, built these rich houses and revitalized the area around Jackson Square. My kind of woman.”

“Sounds exactly like you. Except for the fingers.”

Empire chairs and inlaid tables stood elegantly on an oriental carpet against the eight foot tall windows. A crystal chandelier cast its shadows onto a sofa upholstered in striped silk. A more contemporary lamp cast a decisive light over a graceful writing table with Cabriole legs. My kind of room.

“I did some preliminary investigation before you got here,” Bob said and placed his quite enormous feet on a delicate Louis XVI table in front of the sofa.

“This afternoon I went to the last address Ricky gave me,” Bob said. “A dilapidated building off North Rampart. Only one I talked to was Ricky’s neighbor. Woman by the name of Monique.”

“Helpful?”

“Yes and no.”

“T*hat’s* helpful.”

“Okay. Said she hadn’t seen Ricky for a month or so.”

“Who is she?”

“White woman, fortyish, padded hips, none-too-clean looking.”

“You always have luck meeting women.”

“Said she’s the greatest voudou queen in all of New Orleans.”

“Lots of those around,” I said.

“Cats running about everywhere.”

“Black?”

“No, not black, a uniform dusty gray. The house was filthy.”

“And what else did she say about Ricky?”

"Nothing specific but she said she'd ask around. Sounded as if she'd consider a finder's fee."

"Did you offer?"

"Not exactly."

"But you held out hope?"

"Something like that."

"What else did she tell you?"

"Nothing. She suddenly clammed up and told me to leave. Said she had an appointment."

"And you waited across the street to see with whom?"

"No one came. And she stayed put."

"And you've had no other contacts in New Orleans since you got here?"

"None at all."

"So, someone from this Monique's house followed you. And then they got me instead of you," I said. "Punishment by association."

"I apologize."

"Vigilance is no longer your middle name, either?"

"Didn't notice anyone following me. Easy to blend into the crowded streets here."

Bob poured himself a third cup of coffee.

"Fill up your cup?"

"Thanks but no thanks. I'll get all jittery," I said. "Can I tell you something?"

"Sure."

"You make the worst coffee."

Chapter 3

"So, how did it all start?" I said.

"About a month ago I lost touch with Ricky Wilson. He didn't answer my e-mails. Never gave me his phone number."

"And?"

"I checked. There was never a phone installed at the address he gave me," Bob said.

"Maybe he simply decided to move on?"

"Yeah, that was my first thought."

"And your second?"

"A bit more complicated. Gwen Wilson called me to say she'd lost touch with him. Very unusual since he would call her several times a week."

"*He* always called *her*?" I said.

"Apparently."

"Phone cards, then."

"Yeah."

"And your connection to Gwen is?" I said.

"She's Ricky's daughter."

"And you know her well?"

"I've known her a long time," he said.

I can read Bob's face pretty well especially when he squirms.

"And why are you blushing?"

"Don't be an ass."

"You're dating her, aren't you? You're dating a twenty-something."

"Oh, boy."

"You're robbing the cradle," I said.

"Come on, she's almost twenty-nine."

"You're dating her."

"Okay, okay, so what?"

"And you needed *me* here, why?" I said.

"Two heads are better than one." Bob stirred his coffee vigorously. "And we haven't done a case together in donkeys' years."

"Too true. Glad you called," I said and looked more closely at him.

His special agent crewcut was gray and the lines in his face deep. He's been something of a loner since his wife left him. She got tired of his special assignments and found herself a university professor whose only challenge was waiting for tenure. And now Bob was dating an almost twenty-nine year old who missed her father. Could this be a good thing?

"And the third reason?" I said.

"Ah."

"Ah, what?"

"Gwen has hired you."

"What do you mean?"

Bob reached into his pocket and drew out an envelope.

"Here's your retainer. She asked that you put your contract in the mail."

Speech eluded me.

"I'd rather stay out of the picture," Bob said.

"You need me to front for you?"

"Something like that."

I opened the envelope and pulled out the check. Double my usual fee.

"At least you're looking out for my finances," I said. "Okay, I'll do it."

"Thanks." Bob pulled out another envelope. "Here, your contract ready to sign and mail. I put a stamp on the envelope."

"You think of everything." I signed and handed the envelope back.

"What do your contacts at the Bureau have to say?" I said. "And don't tell me you didn't get in touch with them?"

"I did." Bob looked at me oddly. "Can't figure it out, though."

"Why not?"

"Subtle stonewalling."

"And if anyone knows stonewalling, you do," I said.

"Couldn't see their faces over the phone so I paid a personal visit to the J. Edgar Hoover building."

"And got nowhere?"

"Some people claimed they were on their way out and would give me a call. Never did. Others couldn't recall Ricky's name."

"I take it you finally found a bird who sang?" I said.

Bob laughed but not very happily.

"Old pal in Human Resources. She showed me how Ricky had applied for and received early retirement."

"It was confirmed, then."

"Except, she said, there's no forwarding address just his bank account where they deposit his pension directly."

"And you just happened to glance at the account number?"

"Only got the name of the bank. The Chase. That's as far as she would go."

"I'd say we take a look at Ricky's house," I said.

"I'll pick you up at the Monteleone at six in the morning," Bob said.

"Oh, God, you know I'm not a morning person."

"You will be tomorrow."

Chapter 4

New Orleans, August 9, 2005

We walked down the quiet streets towards North Rampart. Without consulting with each other we'd both changed our appearance. I wore a long denim skirt, a bulky jacket, a head-scarf to conceal my hair, and a pair of granny glasses without prescription lenses. Pseudo-hippie.

Bob had on jeans, a gray sweat shirt over his expanding middle, and a baseball cap pulled far down over his forehead. Don't mess with me his demeanor announced.

Ricky's house looked, if possible, more dilapidated than the buildings surrounding it. Several rails were missing in the fence, two scraggly bushes and a small flowerbed were in immediate need of water. The street was empty, and no one stirred in the houses.

We went to the narrow space between the neighbor's house and Ricky's and circled around to the back.

"Damn, only one entrance," Bob said.

"The front door it is," I said.

I got out my key ring and pulled off the lock picks I keep handy for occasions like this.

"Stand behind me," I said. "Look like you belong."

I crouched down and rattled the lock. It was brand new. The very first pick went in as if through butter. I jiggled it a few times, heard the click and, presto, opened the door. Never happened that easy before. Ever.

"Boy, you're good," Bob said and pushed me inside.

My lock-picking skills come from one of Bob's more unsavory friends. Hank is a former convict in whose basement in Virginia I had practiced for several weeks picking locks, easy ones at first, then graduating to increasing degrees of difficulty. After a month Hank declared proudly that I could pick any lock currently in existence.

"Wonder who owns the house," I said when we stood in the small front room. It was clean of decor. No books, no magazines, no paper plates with left-over pizza. The air was fetid and one sad plant hung dead on the coffee table.

The sofa and three chairs were white rattan with grubby pillows. I tossed the pillows on the floor. Nothing. I ran my hands along the inside of the furniture and stubbed my fingers on the rough branches. The small glass vial was wedged into the side of the third chair.

"He's on drugs," I said.

"No, he isn't."

"What would you call this?"

"A vial without a label."

"I'll send it to Washington," I said. "Got a clean sandwich bag?"

"No, but I've got Kleenex."

I wrapped up the vial and put it in my pocket.

We could hear water dripping in the kitchen. One every second like clockwork with a sharp pling on metal.

"I'll take the bedroom. You take the kitchen," Bob said, the kitchen in his mind being woman's work. But I forgive him.

The faucet was stuck and the water kept dripping no matter how hard I turned the handle. There was hardly anything in the cupboards and the refrigerator yielded a few wilted vegetables. The pots and pans were in the sink as if someone had planned to return to do them. Or not.

"What've you got," Bob shouted.

"Nothing."

"Nothing in here either. Just a single sock under the bed."

I joined Bob in the bedroom.

"Looks as if he left in a hurry," I said.

"Yeah, didn't have time to close the drawers. But everything is gone."

"Let's look at the bathroom and then leave," I said.

The door was stuck as if the wood had warped and filled the frame too tight. Bob put a shoulder to it.

We both knew the source of the foul-smelling air that poured out of the room and enveloped us. I clapped a hand over my mouth and nose but the stink was too overpowering.

"Dead body," I said.

Bob pushed aside the shower curtain and we stared into the bathtub.

"Two," he said.

The rats had been caught in huge traps, tossed in the tub, and abandoned. They were in an advanced stage of decay.

"Let's get out," Bob said.

"We need to search the cabinets," I said.

The cabinet above the sink was empty. No needles. No vials. The same went for the single cupboard under the sink. Just a roll of toilet paper and an unopened bottle of disinfectant.

We left on the point of retching, shut the bathroom door tightly and crossed the front room.

Bob looked up and down the street before we stepped outside.

"Phew," he said.

"What do you make of it?" I said.

"What I make of it is that Ricky left no clues about his new life. That he took his drums with him. That he didn't eat or drink here—there was nothing in the kitchen."

"And he didn't sleep here," I said. "There were no sheets on the bed, no pillows."

"And he didn't like rats and had them assassinated," Bob said. "I could have told you that last bit. He has a thing about vermin."

"Like who doesn't."

"Except for the rats the house was sanitized," Bob said.

"And except for the vial."

"There's got to be an explanation."

"What? Vitamin B?"

"Could be."

"Come on," I said.

"You don't know Ricky. A straight-shooter if ever there was one." Bob looked truly upset.

"I'll send the vial UPS," I said. "Overnight."

"Fine."

We started walking.

"What's your plan now?" Bob pulled off his baseball cap. I took off the granny glasses.

"Follow me. We need breakfast," I said. "And then introduce me to Ricky's neighbor, Monique."

Chapter 5

Her house was on a corner opposite St. Louis Cemetery #1.

Bob knocked on the door and after about three minutes it opened a slit.

The Venerable Monique was disheveled and looked as if she'd had a rough night. Her cats clustered around her feet in the doorway and she closed the door a fraction more.

"Go to the City of the Dead," she said after she'd stared at Bob's face long enough to recognize him. "Until I wake up. They open at nine." And she shut the door.

"The City of the Dead? What the heck does she mean?" Bob looked irritated.

"She means the cemetery," I said. "Across the street."

The tops of vaults with figures of saints were visible above a long white-washed wall. A tall winged statue with a huge cross rose up in the middle.

"And I suppose you're now going to give me one of your travel agent tours?"

"If you like," I said. "That's one of my many talents and I *did* read up on it when I was here last year."

"Fine. Okay. If you must, you must."

We crossed the wide boulevard and joined an excitable group of tourists clustered around the gate. It was locked. Their guide fluttered about, bewildered, until a jeep pulled up and a city worker came to the rescue with a bundle of keys. Bob and I waited until the group disappeared inside and turned right. We took a left.

"Welcome to the City of the Dead," I said.

The pavement between the ancient tombs and once-splendid mausoleums was crumbling and so were many of the walls of the vaults. Some family names had all but disappeared. Only the black wrought-iron fences had withstood the ravages of time.

"Okay," Bob said. "Give me the tour."

"Fine. See this outer brick wall and the square vaults. Called "oven" vaults."

"Sounds ominous."

"Too true. Originally the poor could be buried here for a fraction of the cost. The vaults were called ovens because the tropical sun baked the remains behind the brick."

"See what I mean?"

"Today the wall is more of a waiting room if the family tomb is full."

"What do you mean, full?"

"It happens in the best of families."

"Not in mine, it doesn't."

"Anyway, one year and one day after burial the last body in the mausoleum is "bagged" and put in the cool basement to make room for the one in the wall."

"Why the one day?"

"Out of respect. They won't bag you on the anniversary of your death."

"You're depressing me."

"The reason the graves are above ground is that in the 1800s the city had no drainage system and the coffins tended to float away."

"Thank you," Bob said. "Are the tombs still in use? The cement around those two last ones looks new."

"I heard they have maybe twenty burials a year, that's all."

"And what's this," Bob said as I led him around a corner and stopped in front of a tall tombstone almost completely covered with blue Xs scribbled in crayon. At the foot of the stone were dried flowers.

"Marie Laveau's tomb. The most famous of all New Orleans voudou queens. She's buried here as the widow Glapion, the man with whom she had fifteen children."

"It looks neglected."

"Well, she died in 1881. Maybe there are no living relatives to take care of the place."

"You'd have thought there were a few descendants from her fifteen kids."

"You'd think so. All I know is that one daughter of the same name succeeded her so it seemed as if Marie Laveau lived supernaturally for a couple of hundred years."

"Was the first Marie born here?"

"Yes. She was a free woman of color, part black, part white, and part Indian. She became the Widow Paris when her first husband disappeared. He was followed by Louis Glapion, the one who fathered her fifteen children."

"How did she become so powerful?"

"Hers was a strange world. More French than American. Creole society was full of unhappy marriages, unhappy women, beautiful quadroon mistresses living in houses bought for them by Creole men who'd married white women for the sake of propriety."

"Sounds decadent."

"Don't know about that. But lots of jealousy, underhanded actions, calls for supernatural interventions. Marie Laveau was a hairdresser—and you know about women and their hairdressers."

"No, what about them?"

"Women tell their hairdressers everything."

"Do you?"

"Of course not. In any case, Marie listened to gossip and used her knowledge to cast her magic spells."

"Magic spells?"

"Exactly. She was smart as a whip. She transformed a primitive cult into a business. She kept the fanatical aspects of voudou—the snake, black cats, drinking the blood of roosters, the sexual orgies at the end of the ceremonies. She was famous for her spells to help rejected lovers, get rid of jealous wives. Or getting a new house for herself."

"Sounds like your kind of woman."

"Very funny. She held public court down in Congo Square by Lake Pontchartrain. She would come swaggering along and, in the middle of the square, bring out her snake from a box and dance with it. And there were private orgies."

"Was she the only voudou queen?"

"No, but the others faded away or were coerced into serving her. I tell you, whoever proclaims herself a voudou queen today pales."

Bob stared with renewed interest at Marie Laveau's tomb. The cemetery was eerily quiet, the muted voices of the tourist group hardly reached us and when the gravel crunched under someone's feet we were both startled.

The man fit right into the cemetery environment. His face was hung about with wild gray hair, his bushy eyebrows dwarfed his pale eyes. His eyelashes were yellow and his skin sickly white.

"Ahem," Bob said, and I moved a few steps away.

"Oh, hello, there, didn't mean to startle you," the man said and sounded so normal that I shook off my first impression. Apparently the same happened to Bob. Though he looked as bland as only he knows how.

"Came by to place a little something at the feet of Marie Laveau. It's my birthday and she sometimes grants wishes," he said and dispelled the relief I had just experienced.

"She grants wishes?" Bob said.

"Yes, there's more between heaven and earth than we mortals can ever know." The man sounded every bit as normal—had it not been for his strange exterior—as did Bob. "My name is Doc Winnipeg."

"I'm Bob Makowski and this is Jamie Prescott," Bob said after a short pause during which I knew he was rooting around for some fake names but couldn't come up with any. Not that there was any need for concealment. He can't help it. It's in his blood.

"Ah," Doc Winnipeg said. "You're not from around here. Let me guess. East coast?"

"Yeah," Bob said and started walking.

Doc Winnipeg followed close on Bob's heels with me bringing up the rear. We trooped in this fashion towards the exit.

Outside the cemetery I fully expected to lose Doc Winnipeg when we walked towards Monique's house. But he stayed right with us until we got there.

He looked amused when I knocked on the door and Monique opened it. He bypassed the two of us, stepped inside, gave her a smart slap on the butt and disappeared.

"You've met, I see," Monique said.

Chapter 6

Her head was in a bandana tied on top and her face was so plump that it was impossible to read anything into it.

Bob straddled a wooden chair and I stayed on my feet so I could roam around.

"You're back," she stated and Bob nodded while I managed a peek behind a curtain and saw a bathroom. A bathroom opening directly into the living room just separated by a curtain?

"Any news of Ricky?" Monique said.

I took a couple of steps to my right past a dirty window and looked behind yet another curtain, this one in front of a room with an altar filled with lit candles and a small grouping of *gris-gris* bags. Doc Winnipeg stood in front of the altar inhaling deeply. The smoke wafted towards me and I wondered he didn't choke and pass out. I nearly did.

"No news yet," Bob said, "but I'd like to ask you a few more questions."

"How do I know you are benevolent?" Monique closed her eyes briefly. "The spirits have not yet spoken to me about you."

"Yeah, well, happens to me all the time," Bob said and showed her his Washington, D.C. licence which he kept in his wallet next to his expired FBI credentials.

"How can you be a special agent and a private investigator at the same time?" she said and opened her eyes as wide as her heavy eyelids allowed. Ah, quick on her feet.

"I'm quite legitimate," Bob said.

Doc Winnipeg came back from communing with the candles. He'd changed into a natty gray suit with a red tie. It helped his mad scientist image somewhat but his hair could not be tamed. It stood in electrified glory all around his head. He sat down opposite Bob at which point I sat down, too, on the only available seat: a low divan infested with cats.

"We understand that you are looking for our good neighbor, Ricky. And now we also understand that this is an official investigation, is that correct?"

Listens behind curtains, I thought.

"Or maybe semi-official?" he continued. "Either way, we don't mind, do we my dear Monique?"

She shook her head.

Neither Bob nor I reacted.

"Let me start at the beginning," Doc Winnipeg said and inspected his fingernails. "We met Ricky when he came here several months ago."

"Six," Monique said.

"About that." Doc didn't look as if he enjoyed being interrupted.

"Ricky plays the drums. He got interested in my collection of African drums," Monique said.

"We were happy to introduce him to our community of worshipers," Doc said.

"Where did Ricky play his drums," I asked.

"Somewhere on Bourbon Street, wasn't it my dear?" Doc Winnipeg looked pointedly at Monique who nodded. "Yes, on Bourbon Street," he repeated and got up.

"You're leaving?" Monique said. "Where are you going?"

"I'm going out."

Doc Winnipeg shook Bob's hand and blew mine a kiss. Monique turned her cheek away when he got to her.

We sat in silence until we heard the front door slam.

"Fuck you!" Monique blared. "He's on his way to see that fake Haitian Priestess, Antoinette."

"Who's Antoinette?" I said.

"An impostor," she said. "Ricky couldn't stay away from her either." Monique stared at me funny from under her heavy eyelids.

"In what way?"

"She let him be a *tambourier* and play the sacred drums although only the initiated are allowed to celebrate the cult of the *loa*."

"Okay," I said. "Ricky is a drummer and what's more natural than to be interested in drums?"

"The drum is a sacred object and should only be handled by initiates. Antoinette violates her ritual obligations. I've heard it rumored that he has been allowed to put the drum to bed and even to feed it."

"Feed a drum and put it to bed?"

"The drums are divinities and must be fed, then they must rest."

"Ooo-ah," Bob wheezed and his eyes rather bulged before he recovered. "And what is Doc Winnipeg's connection to Haiti?" he said.

"Nero is a great, benevolent doctor."

"He's a real doctor?" I said.

"Of course, he is."

"And his first name is Nero?"

"That's right. Dr. Nero Winnipeg."

"Where is his practice?"

"He is the head of the volunteer organization, *Cliniques d'Haiti*, you must have heard of them. They do great work for the poor." Monique handed me a pamphlet printed on inferior paper.

A quick glance through the brochure told me that the non-profit organization had been in business since 2002, that their volunteers had helped hundreds of Haitian children in need of medical attention. The photographs were eloquent with pathetic staring eyes imploring the prospective donor to give just a dollar a day to keep the doctor away. I looked in vain for a pie-chart showing how the funds were being distributed.

"Now," Bob said. "You last saw Ricky about a month ago?"

"That's right."

"Did he say anything about giving up his rented house?"

"I didn't know he'd done that. I thought he went back up north for a visit. I was a bit surprised he didn't say goodbye." Monique shrugged. "But then, you can't count on anyone anymore."

Ain't that the truth, I thought.

"Do you know with whom he hung out?" I said.

"Not really."

"And you don't know where on Bourbon Street he played?"

"Not really. Those musicians roam from place to place."

Bob looked at me and I looked at Bob. End of the line.

"Here." I gave Monique my card with my cell phone number and the number to the Hotel Monteleone on the back.

"Will you call me if anything comes up?"

"Sure thing," Monique said and got up, obviously eager to see us go.

We walked back down to Royal Street and got caught up between groups of tourists and sidewalk musicians. There were three of the latter and they had arrived on bicycles. They had set up a small stand with CDs for sale and a shoe box where coins and bills barely covered the bottom. The tuba player and the woman with the tambourine were black. The saxophonist was an older white guy. No drums.

"Can't imagine Ricky doing that," Bob said.

"Does Ricky play any other instruments apart from the drums?" I asked. "I know musicians can be versatile."

"No idea. It seems I don't know squat about him anymore."

We stopped near Jackson Square.

"About Doc Winnipeg. Will you investigate or shall I?" I said.

"I'll let you handle it."

"Fine," I said. "What's your bet?"

"If he's really a doctor then he's not an MD. Maybe a PhD kind of doctor, if that."

"My thoughts exactly."

"Could we be wrong?"

"Yes, we could," I said. "Look, I'll hit the bar scene tonight. I'm thinking of taking Bourbon Street from one end to the other showing Ricky's photo. How about you?"

"I'll get a hold of my contact in Human Resources at the Bureau in Washington. I need Ricky's bank account number. Then to the Chase to get a print-out and see what's going on in his account. And I'll show Ricky's photo at the bank and around Jackson Square."

"Let's bake it and shake it and see what happens," I said. "Let's visit a Voudou Temple."

Chapter 7

Her ad was on page 97 of the New Orleans travel guide.

Visit the authentic Voudou Temple of Priestess Antoinette. Ritual cleansing. Healing and Power. Spiritual knowledge. Powerful Voudou spells. Gris-gris bags. Voudou dolls, candles, and Haitian art. Gain prosperity and peace.

The temple was in the French Quarter.

We stood in the street in front of a house painted dirty ochre. The stucco had peeled off in large patches exposing the structure as wooden beams and bricks. A hand-made sign with a wiggly arrow pointed down a walkway towards the back.

The passage was wider than I'd first thought. At the back three wooden steps led to a porch with two red bannisters decorated with white curlicues. I knew instantly what they were.

"*Vévés* as in voudou," I said to Bob. "The signs that will make the spirits, or *loa*, appear."

"If you say so," he said.

Half a dozen painted wood panels sprang into colorful view at the top of the stairs. Human skulls with protruding teeth and empty eye-sockets. A voudou queen in front of white tombstones. A snake—likely Damballah, the serpent god—curled around the top of a large cross. And a white rooster looking lost without its head.

"What the hell," Bob said.

The door stood ajar and squeaked when I pushed it open. We entered.

"Hello?" I said.

And again, "hello?"

The space inside was dark.

Not exactly a souvenir shop. Not exactly a voudou temple. More of a museum. Glass shelves crammed with faceless fabric dolls. Vévé-decorated candles in all sizes and colors and baskets with *gris-gris* bags. Small glass bottles filled with colored powders and some with cloudy liquids. And, on the floor, a large collection of African drums. Tall, small, squat, oblong.

The woman startled me. She could have been observing us since we entered. She was half hidden by a curtain which covered a doorway to the back. She was beautiful and ebony black. Large almond-shaped eyes, high tits, slim hips.

"Oh," I said and my heart skipped a beat.

"Ah," Bob breathed.

"Are we trespassing?" I said to the woman. "We thought this was a souvenir shop."

She didn't move. Her enormous eyes glinted in the dim light, her nostrils were wide, and her lips full.

"What you lookin' for?" She stepped forward, bare feet in sandals.

I pointed randomly to the *gris-gris* bags in the basket. They were the size of oranges, wrapped in red flannel, tied with black string.

"How much are those?" I said.

"Not for sale," she said.

"Rude as hell," Bob muttered under his breath.

"How about a voudou doll," I said and pointed to one with a vacant face, in a checkered dress with formless feet dangling underneath.

"Not for sale. I close now. We do not sell," she said and moved towards us. I felt a whiff of exotic perfume in the air and caught a movement behind her. Bob was fast on his feet and moved towards the back of the store while I pulled out my wallet and took out Ricky Wilson's photograph.

"Looking for a friend of mine," I said. "Recognize him?"

She glanced at the picture for less than a second and shook her head.

"His name is Ricky Wilson and I'm told he comes here to play the drums," I said.

Bob pulled aside the curtain at the doorway towards the back.

"Doctor," he exclaimed. "What a surprise."

Doc Winnipeg's hair flowed wildly around his face. He stared stony-faced at Bob and held up a humongous candle.

"You do get around," he said. "Antoinette, these folks are friends of Ricky's. Maybe you remember him?"

"Not really," she said.

"I'm not surprised. He was a strange guy. Wanted to play your drums."

"No one plays my drums," she said.

"Exactly," Doc Winnipeg said to Bob. "I told you Ricky hasn't been around for a long time."

"But now you recognize him?" I said to Antoinette and held out Ricky's photograph again.

"I do not."

"Fine," I said. "Bob, we should be leaving."

"How much are the drums?" Bob said.

"They are not for sale," Antoinette shouted. She went rapidly to the front door, opened it and pointed us outside.

"Goodbye," Doc Winnipeg said. "And good luck with your search."

"Good luck my foot," I said to Bob when we were on the sidewalk. "What else did you see behind the curtain?"

"Drums stacked from floor to ceiling. Hundreds of candles."

"And?"

"And the back of a very slim guy—in a bright yellow shirt—disappearing through a back door."

Chapter 8

New Orleans, August 10, 2005

We were at the Café Du Monde sitting cheek to jowl with the early evening crowd. Best meeting place in New Orleans. Open 24/7 except for Christmas Day and hurricanes. Fast service, no menu. Just café-au-lait and beignets. With mountains of powdered sugar.

The harried servers swung loaded trays above our heads and fumes of chicory hung under the green-and-white-striped awning. Tourists galore. Women in pink tee shirts and cropped pants. Men in plaid Bermudas and black socks in sandals.

"No place like this," I said. "Established in 1862."

"Some place. Best damn coffee I ever had," Bob said. "Chicory. Whatever that is."

"Chicory root, roasted, grown right here," I said. "Goes back to the civil war when coffee was scarce. Chicory root was added to eke out the supply. Then they kept the blend for the smooth flavor."

"Now how did I know you knew?"

"You know me too well," I said. "What did you accomplish this afternoon?"

"I went to the Chase and talked to the manager. She took a hard look at my FBI identification and although I don't think she suspected anything she still insisted on verifying my credentials with someone in Washington."

"Good for her."

"Yeah, hip-hip hurrah for her," Bob said.

"And you had her call your contact in Human Resources who has been conditioned to vouch for you?"

"Of course. I've got her over a barrel. She has already compromised herself by showing me Ricky's file."

"I bet she's getting nervous."

"Nah. She declared me a *bona fide* agent and the bank manager was putty in my hands."

"So, let me guess, you got printouts of Ricky's statements. What did they show?"

"His pension has been withdrawn in cash like clockwork on the second day of each month. No checks have been written on the account."

"So, where does that leave us?"

"Wait, there's more. I returned to the bank after looking at the last two statements. Seems the full amount is now being transferred automatically to another bank."

"And you obtained the name of the bank?"

"The bank manager—my new best pal—furnished me with the information. The Hibernia National Bank."

"You have a wonderful way with women."

"Yes, I know. The next step was not that complicated. She had a confidential conversation with her opposite number at Hibernia and came up with the names of Ricky Wilson and Brandy Gregory. Two home addresses one of which was Ricky's. The other was 3200 Baronne Alley. Joint account."

"Ricky must have been present with this Brandy Gregory in order to open the account. Their signatures must have been notarized. Did you go to the Hibernia Bank to verify?"

"Sure thing. Couldn't get printouts, though."

"But you found the notary public and showed her Ricky's picture?"

"The notary resigned last month."

"And you got her address?"

"She's moved away. Hardly worth pursuing."

"End of that line."

"Exactly. What are you thinking?"

"I'm thinking that if Ricky has disappeared and his money is being transferred to a joint account, who's getting the money? Who is this Brandy Gregory?"

"That's for us to wonder and for you to find out."

"Okay," I said and wrote down the address.

"What do you know about this voudou mumbo-jumbo?" Bob said and twirled his coffee around in the mug.

"There's no shortage of voudou priestesses, both black and white, in New Orleans," I said. "You want the long story or the short?"

"As much as I need to understand what's going on."

"Okay. You'd probably spell it *voodoo* but others prefer *vodu* or *voudou* to get away from the black magic image."

"Fine with me. What is it exactly?"

"Voudou means god or divinity but the concept includes the rites, the sacred objects—the rattles, the drums, the amulets—and the *hunsis* who are the servants of the spirits."

"Spirits?"

"Or gods. Damballah, the snake, is one of the most powerful."

"Sounds Freudian."

"And you know all about Freud," I said. Sometimes Bob's not half bad.

"I'm not entirely ignorant."

"Its power is revealed only through the priest and priestess called the *houngan* and the *mambo*. That's it in a nutshell," I said. "Not what we understand by a religion."

"Where did it start ?"

"In Africa. Brought to Saint Domingue—that's Haiti today—with the slaves from Dahomey and Nigeria in the early 1700s. That's when it merged with symbols from the Catholic religion."

"And how did voudou get to New Orleans?"

"Not so fast," I said.

"Okay, if you must, but give it to me in small doses."

"I'll take you back to the French Revolution of 1789 and all the talk about *liberté, egalité* and *fraternité*."

"Oh, no."

"Oh, yes. There were five hundred thousand blacks in Saint Domingue. They mistakenly assumed that what was freedom, equality, and brotherhood in France meant the same for them."

"Always thought there was something fishy about the French Revolution." Bob smiled at me. He fails to understand my deep affection for all things French and seizes any opportunity to needle me.

"When it dawned on them that they were still considered second class they set about to massacre the white plantation owners."

"Didn't know that," Bob said.

"They were led by a former slave, Toussaint Louverture, and his commander, Dessalines. They were successful until Napoleon Bonaparte sent his navy across the seas to suppress the uprising."

"Napoleon used to be my hero," Bob said.

"Well, history is in the eye of the beholder."

"He was so cool with the triangular hat and his hand inside his jacket. Imperial."

"They say he was scratching at an eczema."

"They'll say anything once you've failed."

"But to get back to Toussaint. Some of his men surrendered, and Toussaint himself was kidnapped and sent to his death by starvation in a French prison."

"Phew," Bob said. "News to me."

"Your hero, Napoleon, at work. But it gets better. The French lost first their troops and then their general, Leclerc, to yellow fever. In 1804, Dessaline stuck it to Napoleon and crowned himself the first black emperor."

"Good for him," Bob said. "Never heard of that either."

"Dessaline tore out the white and blue sections of the Tricolor and created a Haitian flag of red and black."

"Blood and death. How long did he last?"

"Not long. And his successors never have, either. It's as if there's a curse on that country. The people either get crushed by their own dictators or "liberated" by foreign powers."

"I seem to remember we were one of those foreign powers."

"Never did anyone any good."

"I'm still waiting for voudou to arrive in New Orleans," Bob said.

"So you are," I said. "After 1804, a prohibition to import slaves from Saint Domingue to Louisiana was lifted and that's when white planters arrived in New Orleans. Their slaves brought voudou with them and it took hold."

"And, obviously, it's still going strong," Bob said.

"Lots of charlatans around today. They succeed because of the gullible souls ready to give donations and pay for consultations and so-called bone readings. They profess to be the bearers of the truth. People attend their healing ceremonies and buy the potions and powders and voudou dolls and *gris-gris* bags."

"Casting spells?" Bob said. "What's in those bags, anyway."

"Probably bones from a black cat skinned seconds after being scalded to death. Strands of human hair. Noxious herbs. Lizard eggs."

"Please, I've just been eating."

"Well, you asked."

"We'll need to go back tomorrow," Bob said. "I'm getting anxious. Let's meet here for breakfast. How's eight?"

"Fine," I said. "You say Ricky played jazz with a group in the French Quarter. Any idea which group and where they played?"

"Not a clue. Somehow I don't see Ricky as a professional musician.

"Look across the street," Bob said. "The guy in the yellow shirt leaning on a lamppost. To your left."

His silk shirt stretched tightly across his chest and abs. His black pants clung equally close and he wore pointy-toe boots with three-inch heels. His features were obscured by dreadlocks. He flicked casual ashes from a cigarette and looked up and down the street but never at us.

"Looks Haitian. Has no surveillance technique," I said.

"Looks like the guy from Antoinette's. Just keep an eye out. He can only follow one of us. We'll split up when we leave."

"I have an idea," I said.

"No, you don't." Bob peered at me suspiciously.

"Trust me. I won't do anything you wouldn't do."

"I know. That's what worries me."

We got up and Bob crossed the street and passed by the lamppost. Slim-Jim experienced a moment of indecision glancing at me still at the café before he flicked his cigarette butt into the gutter and followed Bob towards Jackson Square. I knew Bob would lead him a small chase before losing him.

I took the low road to the French Quarter and the jazz clubs.

Chapter 9

Jake's Jazz Club was located on a choice corner of Bourbon Street. I'd stopped by here every night during my Mardi Gras vacation in The Big Easy last year.

Live music, laughter, and shouts spilled into the street from the jazz club. Jake was behind the bar and did a double-take when he recognized me. He glanced briefly at my blue cheek which I had more or less covered with concealer make-up. Couldn't do much about the nose.

"Table for two?" he said.

"No, Jake, a seat for one at the bar where I can talk to you."

"How you bin?" His grin was infectious. He has a way with women and I have a way with bartenders.

"I've been good," I said, "though I've not enjoyed any real jazz since I was here last. Any chance of Henry Butler or Lars Edegren showing up here tonight?"

"None of those. But someone equally good."

"Yeah?"

"The Jon Douglas Stompers. They rock."

Three of the four Stompers, the furry-faced bass player, the long-haired pianist, and the balding drummer were already in place when Jon Douglas arrived. What I didn't see was anyone looking like Ricky Wilson.

The atmosphere became charged. The packed room stood to attention and the applause was loud even before he raised the sax to his lips and let the first mellow tones float on the air.

“Get you a Hurricane?” Jake asked.

“Sure, the perfect after-dinner drink,” I said and remembered I hadn’t had dinner.

At certain intervals people would shout out their approval and Jon would sway slightly in their direction without losing his concentration.

“Is that a John Coltrane piece?”

“Sure,” Jake said. *“Cousin Mary* and the next one will be *Shiny Steps.* The Stompers play traditional.”

“Intellectuals,” I said and Jake grinned.

“What’s with *them*?” I said when he came cruising back from serving an impressive group of guys in tees with cut-off sleeves. Their chests and arms and a few necks were totally tattooed, snakes and flowerbeds and scaly fish everywhere and one sad-looking Madonna. The real kind with a halo. I glimpsed a nipple with a ring, an earlobe with a zircon, a rock punk hairdo.

“Just traveling through,” Jake said.

“Thank God,” I said. “When does the band take a break?”

“Ten minutes.”

I was beginning to droop. The bar stool was uncomfortable. I was contemplating my next move when the music stopped and Jon Douglas pushed his way towards the bar high-fiving members of his audience in passing.

“The usual,” he said to Jake and turned around to look at me.

His forehead was sweaty, his straight black hair swept back below his ears. His eyes were deep Irish blue with black lashes and his skin had an alabaster look to it. He was six feet tall and well put together. He also looked about twenty years old but, on second thought, I amended this to thirty-ish. It was actually hard to tell in the dim light.

What I did notice was the frank way he stared at me.

"What?" I said.

"What happened? Someone beat you up?"

"No, I ran into a door."

"Ah," he said and put his hand lightly on my arm, his eyes glinting.

"Some door."

"Revolving."

"You should be careful about the doors you hang out with."

"I'll try to do better."

"In town for long?"

His hand was still in close proximity.

"A week."

"Good."

My arm felt like lead. I looked across to the tattooed guys.

"Thinking of getting a tattoo?" Jon asked.

"No, just looking."

"Maybe a little red heart."

"Why, do *you* have one?"

"Not a heart."

"Oh?"

"I'll show you when you've looked through my collection of etchings."

"Oh, please," I said. "Hand me a better line. As it happens I've got more urgent things on my agenda."

"What could be more urgent?"

"Looking for a friend of mine," I said.

"What kind of friend?"

"A drummer by the name of Ricky Wilson," I said and tried to shake off the heat that had shot down my spine at his touch.

"Ricky Wilson?" he said.

"Ever heard of him?"

He shifted his weight and moved his hand away.

"Who wants to know?"

"My name is Jamie," I said. "Ricky's a friend of a friend of mine who told me to look him up if I was ever in New Orleans. I'm here and I thought I'd say hi to him."

Jon Douglas put down his glass on the counter and waved to his Stompers who were back at their instruments. He turned his back to me and started walking but just before he was out of earshot he said over his shoulder:

"Ricky Wilson? Doesn't ring a bell. Sorry."

Jake was eyeing me trying to pretend he hadn't overheard our conversation. Of course he'd heard every word. That was his job as bartender.

"And you," I said sternly. "Have you run into him in the last six months?"

I pulled out Ricky's photograph and kept it under Jake's nose. He stopped wiping the counter long enough to glance at the image and to shake his head.

"No, no, I don't know him," Jake said and wouldn't let me pay for my drinks when I got up to leave. "But if I do hear something where can I reach you?"

"I'm at the Monteleone."

"Until when?"

"Don't know exactly. I guess until I've talked to Wilson," I said. "Call me, will you?"

"Sure thing, darling."

At the front door I half turned and caught Jon Douglas watching me. He dipped, then lifted, his saxophone and smiled at me with his eyes only. Heat shot back down my spine.

Chapter 10

"Ever see this guy?"

I was at the carousel piano bar at the Monteleone—where the bar actually rotates slowly, slowly, to the confusion of the already pickled brains of the late drinkers. I'd shown Ricky's photograph at six more bars on my way back without results.

The bartender gave the picture a brief look.

"Don't think so," he said.

"It's important."

"Sorry. What can I serve you?"

"A Mimosa," I said.

He served my drink and I sat there turning and turning. The clientele here was of a different ilk from the one I'd left behind at *Jake's*. No tattoos here. A couple of hefty men in jackets and ties mulling over some sales slips. A woman in a black evening gown with a white gardenia twirling her glass around and waiting. Four golfers in plaid pants and crocodile shirts. I was about to walk off when the bartender beckoned to me.

"Show me that picture again."

He brought the photo across to a better light.

"Maybe."

He put it way up to the bulb.

"Could be. A guy came in last week and sat at the back with one drink the whole night. Just staring into it. Looked like an insurance salesman, kinda faded and gloomy."

"Are you pretty sure or only maybe sure?"

"Pretty sure. Yeah, that might be him."

I sat down and ordered another Mimosa, not that I needed one.

"It's really important," I said. "Are you quite sure?"

"Now it has to be quite sure, not just pretty sure?"

"Would be good."

"I'm as sure as anyone can be in this place."

"Thanks a bunch. I appreciate your effort."

I left a good tip and took back the photograph. Then I went to the registration desk and showed the photograph to the tired night clerk.

"Ever see this guy?"

As clerks go he was all right but his memory must have been blurred by the hundreds of faces which had come his way over time.

"Don't know. Don't think so." he said and sank back behind the counter.

The Monteleone is not located on Royal Street. No, it's on Rue Royale and is a four star hotel. The facade is gorgeously decorated with stucco ornamentation and the inside matches. White squared marble floors, potted palms, Chinese urns with fresh flowers. The suites have evocative names such as the Hemingway, Faulkner, Tennessee Williams, and Eudora Welty suites. My junior suite was nothing to sneeze at, either. It doesn't hurt that there's a heated pool and a fitness room on the top floor. It's well known in certain circles in Washington that I enjoy luxury.

Zooming up in the elevator I contemplated the possibility of breaking into the hotel's registration records to look up Ricky Wilson and decided they were more or less nil.

I called Bob.

"You sound chipper," he said.

"Some jazz and a nightcap revived me," I said.

"I thought that's where you were headed."

"Went to *Jake's Jazz Club* on Bourbon Street. Rowdy place but some good jazz and impressive tattoos."

"Not my cup of tea," Bob said. "But I would've come along anyway."

"I know," I said.

I didn't want to come right out and say it but I really work best alone. Especially in bars.

"Might've enjoyed the tattoos," he said. "Once knew a guy who tattooed his girl friend's name on his chest."

"Ouch."

"When they split up it took him a year to find a new girl with the same name."

"That wouldn't have been you by any chance?"

"I may look like a wild swinger, but no." Bob laughed. "So, what did you find out?"

"I got the feeling that the band leader knew Ricky and that Jake did, too."

"Just a feeling?"

"Kind of. The band leader said he'd never heard of him. Showed Jake Ricky's photo and he said he'd never seen him."

"Which led you to believe the contrary?"

"Yes. And, now don't get excited when I tell you what else I found out. It's probably nothing."

"What?"

"The bartender at the Monteleone—you know at the rotating piano bar—looked at Ricky's picture in the dark and had to think twice."

"What? What did he say?"

"He said he might have seen Ricky last week, drinking alone," I said.

"Last week? But Monique said she hadn't seen him in more than a month."

"I don't know how to explain that," I said.

"Why did he leave his house, then? And where could he be staying instead?"

"I don't know, I don't know. The bartender could be mistaken," I said. "And one more thing. Slim-Jim has been following me around since five this afternoon."

"You've got to deal with him."

"I will."

Chapter 11

New Orleans, August 11, 2005

I caught the early show.

The lights dimmed, two spotlights searched the stage, a drum roll built up, and the show at the *Blues Grotto* swung into action.

I was at a crowded table with a dozen tourists with *Wisconsin Bearhuggers* t-shirts. It was a rowdy, self-serve establishment and I had filled my plate at the buffet with red beans and rice, okra, and shrimp remoulade, balancing a second plate with bread pudding doused in whiskey sauce, and a champagne flute of bubbling fragrant Mimosa. I was set to go.

Jazz is full of soul and pain and yearning and intensity. And this band blasted away with deafening result. The trumpets roared, the trombones bleated, a sax cried. Each took a solo. Then they raised the roof in unison to a frenzy of applause. When the sound dropped to a whisper the acclaim died down.

A spotlight swept across the stage and found the priestess coming in from the wings.

Monique, the Voudou Queen, was magnificent tonight.

She looked nothing like the frumpy woman of yesterday. She was in a sequined white gown and a gold tiara. Her eyelids were heavy and blue with an outrageous sweep of glitter, her lips crimson. She had on dark make-up and it was hard to tell if she was white or black.

She raised the microphone, tossed back her head, waited for the drums to take up the beat from the brass instruments, and belted out a song I didn't recognize. The spotlight followed her around the stage while the band stayed in the dark background.

It had been a simple matter of a call to Washington to discover that Monique was the owner of the *Blues Grotto*, that her last name was Jones, that she was divorced, and that she was on the verge of bankruptcy. I'd left a message for Bob but hadn't heard back from him before leaving for the restaurant.

The search for someone who might recognize Ricky's photo had taken me from Galatoire's to Arnaud's to Pat O'Brien's to the Razoo and the Cat's Meow. After I'd sipped a third of about six drinks I'd hit paydirt.

The bartender at my next to last stop had taken a second and then a third look at the picture.

"Yes," he said. "He was here last week."

"How sure are you?"

"A hundred and ten percent."

"A hundred percent would do it," I said.

And then I'd gone to the last bar before *Jake's* and got the same answer.

"Yes," the bartender said. "He was in last Thursday or maybe four days ago. He was the last customer to leave."

"Are you sure?"

"Do I look like a jester?

"No, sir," I said. He was a mountain of muscle with a belly about to pop the buttons on his brocade vest.

I'd left a second message for Bob.

When the music intensified Monique spun around defying her own bulk until she reached the back of the stage and disappeared into the shadows. Colored lights swept around the stage and lit up first one, then the next musician, until they were all illuminated and I saw them quite clearly.

The lapels and cuffs of their purple jackets were outlined in rhinestones and jiggled as they moved. A group of muscular guys almost as wide as they were tall, with hefty guts and massive thighs. They looked menacing in tinted glasses.

The one with the sweet saxophone was Jon Douglas.

When he stepped to the edge of the stage he stared into the dark audience seemingly straight into my eyes. But this time all I felt was a warning sign in the pit of my stomach and a voice at the back of my head—which could very well be Bob's—warning me to stay away from this bad boy.

Jon stepped back from the edge, raised his sax and set the beat for the band.

Their music was in-your-face. They worked up a sweat and soon they glistened along with the rhinestones. They stomped and twirled as much as their bulks allowed, in fact, they were surprisingly light on their feet. They segued into one number after the other hardly acknowledging the applause. Which was more like a screaming response from the touristy audience.

After their third number the band disappeared and a pianist sat down to accompany Monique. She entered the stage like a queen and bestowed a royal greeting on one and all.

I looked down from my seat in the balcony. The hall was full, the audience enthusiastic, and Slim-Jim was sitting on a bench against the wall where he could keep an eye on me. I felt irritation rise with the bubbles from my half-finished Mimosa.

Monique belted out a tune which made the saints go marching in. And she had the audience in her pudgy hand. She held the stage alone with magnificent poise. Her crimson lips whispered the words. She strode across the stage lightly. I was amazed at her stamina. Where had the dowdy woman in a bathrobe and a bandana gone?

I left the spectacle reluctantly. As the spotlight—and the wild applause—followed Monique back to the wings, I slipped out of my seat, walked downstairs, and found a stage door.

The applause continued and I heard Monique return for her encore. When I looked around Slim-Jim had disappeared.

The stage door was unlocked. There were no guards. Monique would be surprised to see me. Within seconds I was inside a musty corridor leading to a single exit.

Chapter 12

The exit door was locked.

This, normally, is not a problem for me but here I thought it would be prudent to seek a legal entrance. I beat a retreat, reverted to the festivities, and found that Monique had returned to the stage. I circled the hall looking for other doors and ended up at the actual exit to the street.

Next to a small cloakroom I found the door I needed.

There was no one in the foyer and the door was unlocked so I entered. It was dark and however long I stood waiting for my eyes to adjust, they didn't. I brought out my pocket flashlight and pointed it ahead. There was another door on my left with traces of blue paint. The knob turned easily enough. I pushed but the door resisted as if someone had piled sandbags behind it.

I put my shoulder to it and shoved. The sandbags moved reluctantly and I slipped inside through the crack. The sandbags moaned audibly. My flashlight found the body and the bloody face of a man. It took me a second to recognize him.

Jon Douglas turned towards me, rolled back his eyes and passed out. His cheeks were swollen, his nose possibly broken, his hair matted in blood, and he was curled up as if his insides hurt.

I touched his neck. His pulse was rapid but at least it was there. His face was deathly white with deep shadows under eyes and cheekbones but, then, the other times I'd seen him I'd noticed the extreme pallor of his skin.

Turning him on his side elicited more deep moaning. He opened his eyes and looked at me. He shuddered and closed them. A stream of blood gushed from his nose. He coughed and gagged and tried to sit up. I found a light-switch on the wall inside the door. When I flipped it, a weak bulb swung on a wire from the ceiling and spread no light at all.

Jon turned around on his knees and I circled his waist with one arm to hoist him up. He was heavier than I'd expected and he suddenly wrapped his arms around my legs. He smiled a nauseating smile, let go of me, slumped back to the ground, and vomited.

"Where did *you* come from?" he said and wiped blood all over his face. Just as I'd done after my run-in with the thugs in the alley.

"Never mind," I said. "Did you recognize them?"

"Gotta get outta here," he mumbled. "Wanna go home."

"And where's home?"

"Twelve blocks. Down by the levees. Can't walk."

"Fine," I said, "we'll find some transportation."

"My sax, where's my sax?" He slid his arms in frantic circles and crawled along the wall until he found it. He picked it up and cradled it in his arms. His hands were bloody but they were strong and well-groomed as if they were a part of his music.

I could hear echoes of stomping feet, hard applause, and the last assault of the trumpets. The show would be over in minutes and it was now or never. I stepped into the foyer clutching Jon's waist and dragged him across the tiled floor and out the front door.

I'll say this for the French Quarter, no one takes any notice of a bloody face or a seemingly intoxicated man held upright by a six-foot woman in jeans, cowboy boots and a ton of colored Mardi Gras beads. Yes, I thought the boots would have been good for stomping but in fact they now pinched my toes.

"Around the corner. Horse and buggy," Jon mumbled.

It was as he said. An old wagon with a lethargic nag stood waiting around the corner. The driver raised his whip in a tired greeting and waited while Jon made three botched attempts to get aboard. I jumped in behind him.

"Lake Avenue," Jon mumbled.

"Poor nag can't go that far. I go around two blocks for tourists. This ain't a cab, folks."

I got out a fifty and handed it to him.

"Make an exception. Please."

He took a closer look at what he might at first have assumed to be a fiver. Without another word he set the nag in motion, turned the wagon in a wide, slow, circle and set off towards Lake Avenue. It took us fifteen minutes.

Jon variously moaned and retched quietly out the side of the wagon, never letting go of his saxophone. At first I cast cautious looks behind us but saw no one in pursuit.

When we arrived I jumped down first, eased Jon out, and walked him to the door. The house was a two-story shutgun with three concrete steps leading up to a small porch surrounded by iron railing. Jon fumbled and took a key from his pants pocket.

He stumbled to the back of the house after turning on a ceiling light which did nothing much for the front room. Or for the furniture. Early Wal-Mart. Posters tacked to the walls—jazz scenes from smoky bars in the thirties—and a rag rug on the floor.

Jon was splashing water in the bathroom and I sat down on a small daybed. On the opposite wall, under the ceiling, a canoe replete with a paddle was suspended with metal wires.

Jon came back into the room in clean jeans, a white shirt, and two wads of cotton sticking out of his nostrils. The red mark across his cheekbone was turning blue and the bridge of his nose was swollen. And he still looked good especially when, as now, he smiled.

My nose itched, I rubbed it vigorously. My hand came away with a streak of blood. I sniffled and found a Kleenex which I jammed up one nostril.

“Aw, shucks,” Jon said. “Beyond the call of duty.”

“If you say so.” I removed the tissue carefully. “Who did this to you and why?”

“I might ask you the same question.”

“I asked first,” I said. “You having a problem with someone?”

“Not until tonight.”

And that’s when I saw the hatchet—its blade freshly sharpened—leaning against the wall in the far corner.

Chapter 13

Jon grinned.

"You think I'm an axe murderer."

"Don't be silly," I mumbled and dismissed the scenario which had just played out in my over-active brain. Hard to describe how, at the drop of a hat, my thoughts run away with improbable but to me—at the moment—quite plausible ideas. After all, why would anyone keep a sharpened hatchet in his living room?

"It's not unusual. This is hurricane country, remember."

"Yes, I remember."

"People have been known to escape floods by hacking their way through their roofs and getting rescued from there. The axe isn't mine. And the house isn't, either. I rent from a musician friend of mine who's away in Texas until September."

"And the canoe?"

"Not mine, either. But the idea is, you take your backpack, hoist it into the canoe, get it out the door, and paddle yourself to safety."

"Why would there be water flooding the streets?"

"New Orleans is built under sea-level. Did you ever walk along the riverfront? Or the 17th Street Canal?"

"Once."

"Did you notice that you'll be looking *up* at the Mississippi River, *up* at the canals, *up* at Lake Pontchartrain?"

"Yes, it was pointed out to me."

"What do you suppose happens when tornadoes and hurricanes swell the waters?"

"The lake runs over?"

"If the levees don't hold."

"What do you mean?"

"Ever see the levees?"

"Can't say that I have."

"They're nothing but compacted earth. If water flows over the top of the pathetic wall it will wash away the earth. The water will rise within minutes. You'd have a hard time getting to the second floor in time."

"And that's where you'll need the hatchet," I said.

"Yes, it's that or drown."

"The canoe sounds better."

"It does."

"For the life of me I don't see why they don't reinforce the levees."

"Controversial subject. In the 1970s the U.S. Corps of Engineers proposed the so-called Barrier Plan to build lock and flood gates to prevent water from Lake Borgne to enter Lake Pontchartrain."

"And were they built?"

"No. You know how it is. Money. Politics. Environmental concerns. Salinity in the lake. Courts halted construction. The Corps of Engineers went for Plan B instead."

"Which was?"

"To build the levees we have today."

"Hope they hold," I said.

"People here—and that goes for elected officials, too—are a fatalistic bunch. They cross their fingers and hope for the best."

"I imagine people will be told to leave if need be?"

"It's not that simple. Hurricanes are unpredictable and no one is going to hit the panic button until the very last minute. And not everyone has a canoe."

I took a closer look at the canoe. Under what would be the water-line was the top of a Champagne cork plugging up a hole. I touched the cork and it fell out.

"How long does it take for one canoe to fill up with water?" I said.

"Ah, well, I'm not planning to stick around long enough to find out. I'll be gone by the first week of September."

"Where are you going?"

"Back home. I've got a gig lined up at my old haunt in Georgetown."

"As in Georgetown, District of Columbia?"

"Exactly right. What's so funny?"

"Oh, nothing. Before we go into anything else it's about time you tell me what you know about Ricky Wilson."

Jon averted his eyes which had been focused on my face.

"Ricky has sworn me to secrecy," he said. "He says people will be tracking him and asking questions and for us—Jake and me, that is—not to give out any information about him."

Jake, you old so-and-so, I thought.

"Said it could become dangerous and that if he should disappear to call this number and report to someone called Sam. Frankly, it sounded paranoid to me."

Jon pulled out his wallet and showed me a phone number.

"Did you call?" I asked.

"No. I don't think that Ricky has actually disappeared."

"When did you last see him?"

"About a month ago."

"And you didn't find it odd not seeing him for a whole month? Wouldn't that count as a disappearance?"

"Not to me it didn't. I've been in Mobile playing for the last three weeks. Got back two days ago."

"Let me have the number, please."

Chapter 14

He gave me the number reluctantly and I called Bob Makowski's cell phone. When I got his voice-mail I'm sure I sounded frustrated.

"Look, what's going on? I've left three messages of no small consequence and I never hear back from you. I'm at 2407 Lake Avenue down by Lake Pontchartrain with a saxophone player by the name of Jon Douglas from *Jake's Jazz Club* on Bourbon Street. He's actually from Washington, D.C. and usually plays at a jazz club in Georgetown.

"This evening he was assaulted inside Monique's *Blues Grotto* where he plays the early shift, and he now informs me that, hello, he does know Ricky and that he last saw him about a month ago just before he, Jon, went to Mobile."

Jon was staring at me.

"In any case," I said to the voicemail, "here's the phone number for someone called Sam which Ricky gave Jon to call in case he, Ricky, should disappear. Do me a favor and check your messages and call me back."

"Who was *that* and who are *you*?" Jon looked annoyed and snatched back the piece of paper with Sam's phone number.

"That was a friend of mine who's looking for Ricky, and I'm Jamie Prescott, owner of a travel agency in Bethesda." I never tell people I'm a private investigator until I absolutely must. Hampers investigations. People clam up.

"As in Bethesda, Maryland?"

"Yes. Quite a coincidence."

"And that's where you live?" he said looking pleased.

"That's right," I said and didn't know if I felt pleased or not. "And you live in Georgetown?"

"Not exactly, I'm down by Dupont Circle, walking distance to everywhere."

"Where did you learn to play the saxophone?"

"Got my bachelor's at Berklee College of Music in Boston. Classical piano, trombone, and jazz composition. Then my master's at George Mason where I went on to study the alto saxophone before I branched out to tenor."

My God, I thought, he's only twenty-eight. I mentally removed the bad boy label I'd given him earlier. Still, only twenty-eight? On the other hand, if Demi Moore could do it, so could I. Not that I was going to.

Jon looked at the sax he'd rescued from the dark corridor at the *Blues Grotto*. "This isn't just any old sax, it's a Buescher Tenor Sax. I've played it now for more than five years."

Okay, I thought, so maybe he's twenty-nine or close to thirty which sounded a little better but not much.

"It's the ideal jazz instrument," Jon said. "Invented, by the way, in the early 1840s by a Belgian living in Paris. His name was Sax."

"Naturally."

"To me, its tone is sensuous and warm. And now, don't laugh, but since the sax was identified with early jazz which developed in the brothels of New Orleans it was considered so decadent that the Vatican actually condemned it in the early 1900s."

"You're kidding. Why would they bother and which Pope had to sacrifice himself to listen to hours of sensuous saxophone music in order to decide that it was decadent?"

Jon held the sax. "It's made of brass with gold plating, and this mouthpiece is made specifically for jazz. Look at the large tip opening. It allows me to bend the notes. Did you notice the growling effect at the back of my throat and the Benny Goodman sliding technique?"

"I'm afraid I missed the finer points. If I get to hear you play again I'll pay attention."

"Good," Jon said. "So how did you get involved looking for Ricky? Is this guy you called your boyfriend or your husband?"

I hadn't decided exactly how much Jon needed to know about the Ricky Wilson case but I had no hesitation telling him that Bob was not my boyfriend.

"No, there's no boyfriend and there's no husband and I'm in New Orleans mainly to arrange for tour packages for my agency."

As usual I felt uncomfortable fibbing to nice people but, then, it goes with the investigative territory. On the other hand, package tours could be a good idea. I'd have Topsy come up with the names of a couple of agencies I could contact as long as I was here.

Topsy Bannister, my childhood friend, college roommate, travel agency co-owner, and sometime Watson to my Sherlock. I'm the tall blonde with square shoulders. She's the short brunette with curves. She's the one who sets me up on disastrous blind dates.

"How long will you be staying?" Jon said.

"Hard to say yet."

"I'll take you around town. Enjoy dancing?"

"Yes, I do. But to get back to Ricky Wilson, does he play drums at *Jake's* and at the *Blues Grotto* and is he any good?"

"The truth or is he a real friend of yours?"

"The truth."

"Not that good."

"Amateurish?"

"If you want to put it that way."

"How did you get to know him?" I said.

"It must have been about six months ago. I usually come down for Mardi Gras and stay through the spring festivals and Ricky showed up on my first day at *Jake's*. My drummer was late arriving and I took on Ricky as a last minute solution."

"How long did you keep him?"

"Not long. My own drummer showed up after a week or so and I had to let Ricky go."

"What then?"

"Nothing. We'd become friends and just hung out."

"And you introduced him to Monique?"

"Yeah. He got to play at the *Grotto* with me a couple of times," Jon said.

"Funny. Monique never mentioned that Ricky played at her Club. But, then, she never mentioned that she owned a club. What do you make of that?"

"It's not a secret," Jon said shortly.

"That last time you saw Ricky did he say what he was planning to do, was he going to return home?"

"I don't actually know where he's from, he never said, he's a very secretive guy."

"Yes?"

"The last time I saw him that's when he gave me the phone number to Sam."

"And you didn't get concerned that something was about to happen to him?"

"Maybe. But then I went to Mobile and didn't think about it until you showed up at *Jake's* and asked about him. I went around to Ricky's house and discovered he wasn't there. Then Monique told me she hadn't seen him since after I left for Mobile and that people had been coming around asking about him."

That much was true, I thought.

"And you didn't think of calling Sam at that point?"

"Didn't get a chance. I got beat up, remember."

"Recognize anyone?" I said.

"You saw the corridor I was in. Dark as the devil. All I felt was that there must have been two of them. One guy held me and the other punched."

Sounded familiar.

"Say anything?"

"Just' Ricky Wilson.' Like out of some bad movie."

"Couldn't be any clearer, though."

Jon sat down on the daybed next to me. His hand touched mine. Together we stared at the canoe hanging from the ceiling. The wood had dried out and you could see light through the cracks between the boards.

"Anything else you want to tell me," I said.

"Maybe." He turned to look into my eyes.

"I mean about Ricky Wilson," I said.

"No. No, that's about it."

Chapter 15

"Tell me about Antoinette," I said.

Jon moved away from me.

"Why?"

"You do know her, don't you?"

"Maybe."

"Either you do or you don't," I said and got up from the daybed. "She's Haitian, isn't she?"

"Oh, you've met her."

"Very briefly but I have a hunch."

"Okay, what about her?"

"What's your problem? It's not as if I'm asking you to reveal state secrets. I'm simply curious, that's all. She seems mysterious."

"Nothing mysterious about her. That's all an act. I'm not sure where she's from exactly but you could be right. Haiti. Isn't that where voudou came from?"

"More or less. How long has she been here?"

"Two years or so. Has some good shows. Putting Monique out of the voudou business. She's got Toussaint. He walks on red-hot coal. Nasty s.o.b."

"And is he Haitian, too?"

"I imagine so. They came here together. Out of the blue. And set up business. Lots of them around suddenly."

"What's her last name?

"Bazile, I believe.

"And Toussaint's? Or is that his last name?"

"No, his last name is Liautaud, or something like that."

"Are they here legally, do you think?"

"Don't know about him. But she says she was born here."

"Are they married?"

"How the hell would I know? What's this all about?"

"Just curious. You must admit she's interesting. But as a matter of fact, Monique mentioned that Ricky hangs out at Antoinette's place."

"I don't know anything about that."

"Okay."

I moved around the room. I could see dirty dishes piled up in the sink in a very small kitchen. He probably left his clothes strewn on the floor as well. I reminded myself he wasn't that far away from his student days.

"Do you know Paris?" Jon said. "Played jazz in Montmartre last year."

Ah, do I know Paris. That's where I suffered through a few years of marriage to the very French Roger. Remembering his equally French mother still gives me goose bumps. I gave up both of them—but am still in love with Paris.

"Yes, I know Paris," I said. When you were in grade school, I thought. Better not go there.

"Want some cold pizza?" Jon said. "With warm beer?"

"Thanks. I could do with some cold pizza and warm beer right now. Why, this place has no refrigerator or microwave?"

"Both on the blink."

We were digging into the cold pizza and swilling warm beer when someone pounded on the front door.

"Don't open the door. I'm going upstairs to look out the bedroom window," Jon said and disappeared.

"It's a guy," he shouted down the stairs just as I heard Bob Makowski's voice clamoring for me.

I opened the door and let him in.

Chapter 16

"Meet Bob Makowski," I said to Jon. "Bob, this is Jon Douglas, the jazz musician I told you about."

They stared suspiciously at one another. Bob was the first to relax probably relieved to notice Jon's youth whereas it took Jon a little longer. Apparently our body language convinced him that Bob and I were far from being romantically involved even though to some we might sound like an old bickering couple.

"Got your messages," Bob said.

"Why didn't you call me?"

"Came to pick you up. We're going places."

"Where are you going?" Jon asked.

Bob ignored him.

"Sorry to break up your little party," Bob said, "but we really have to push off."

I got up and prepared to leave in order to prevent any further discussion of the whys and wherefores. It was obvious that Bob had new information, that he was in a hurry, and that there was no way he was going to talk in front of Jon.

"Thanks for the pizza and the beer," I said to Jon.

"I'll give you a call tomorrow," he said and glared at Bob.

"Good to meet you," Bob said to Jon and looked as if he didn't mean it. He held the door open, let both of us out, and closed it behind him.

"Here," he said. "I have a rental car waiting around the corner. I'll tell you all about it on the way."

"Okay, shoot," I said while we rolled away to an address I didn't recognize.

"I checked out this Jon Douglas after you called. Seems to be what he told you. Lives at Dupont Circle, plays at a jazz club on M Street in Georgetown, and that's as far as I got."

"No surprise there," I said.

"He's too young for you," Bob said.

"My God, look who's talking," I said. "Surely, what's sauce for the gander etcetera."

"It's not the same thing."

"What, because I'm a woman?"

"No, because you always pick the wrong guys no matter their age."

I ignored him. Unfortunately, he was right.

"As I was about to say," Bob continued, "I showed Ricky's picture to several people in the neighborhood of the Pontalba Apartments and around the shops in Jackson Square."

"Any results?"

"No. And no one at the Café Du Monde remembered him—not surprising seeing how beleaguered the servers are."

"But?"

"But two separate vendors at the flea market said Ricky had been there four or five days ago." Bob looked pleased and confused at the same time. And that's about how I felt, myself.

"That's the information I got at the Carousel Piano Bar," I said, "and later at the bar on Bourbon Street."

"I know."

"What do you make of it?" I said. "Are we chasing someone who doesn't want to be found? He's not gone undercover for the FBI by any chance and we're messing him up?"

"Hardly. My contact in Human Resources was very emphatic. Ricky has retired from the Bureau."

"But you know better than anyone how it works. If he's gone undercover they would make it look real. Did you call the number I gave you?"

"Yes, and you've already guessed it. The number is no longer in service."

"So what do you make of the sightings? If he's in the area we could actually be running into him at any moment."

"We'll know soon enough. We're on our way to the address Brandy Gregory gave the bank."

We were back in the French Quarter. Bob found a parking spot and we got out on the corner of Burgundy and Ursulines with Bob leading the way.

"3200 Baronne Alley," he mumbled and I helped him look for the number until we got to the corner and there were no more houses on that street.

We stood a couple of seconds and looked around in the dark and that's when it all began to look familiar to me.

"Listen," I said under my breath. "This Brandy Gregory obviously gave a fake address to the bank."

"You don't say." Bob sounded his most sour self.

"Bank obviously failed to verify her driver's license."

"Happens," Bob said.

"But all's not lost," I said, "because around the next corner I do believe we'll find the lovely voudou priestess, Antoinette. Might as well go visit as long as we're here."

"Might as well."

"If it's true, as Monique said, that Ricky has been hanging out here we might just find him without any further ado," I said.

And, I added to myself, I could go home and spend some quality time at my house in Bethesda, attend to my neglected travel agency, and mollify Topsy whose e-mails were getting quietly desperate. Since her recent off-and-on separation from Jack, her cheating husband of twenty-three years, she hadn't been her usual optimistic, fun-loving self. I ought to be there for her. We have been better than sisters since we met in first grade at Sidley Friends in Washington.

"Let's go find Ricky," I said fervently.

Chapter 17

When we climbed the stairs to the porch we triggered a flood-light and faster than I'd have given him credit for Bob barreled back down the steps behind me.

"Geez," he whispered.

After that we stayed in the shadows. The moon, if there was one, was hidden behind a low-hanging veil of clouds. There was rain in the air. In the darkness I could just about make out one of the painted wood panels on the wall. The one with the serpent god perched on top of a large cross.

We moved along the side of the porch and came to a wooden fence which creaked and groaned. It was over six feet tall which made it possible for me to stand upright rather than crouch to look through two of the slats. The ground was soggy.

"What's that foul smell?" Bob whispered.

"No idea."

The stink—composed of body odors and some unspeakable rotten stuff—had me hold my nose in order to prevent a violent sneezing attack. Something moved five inches from my face on the other side of the fence and as I scanned the length of it I saw the backs of about a dozen bodies swaying to some internal rhythm and moaning deep in their throats.

Bob moved to the end of the fence and I followed him mainly to get out of my reeking field of observation.

"Here," he whispered and crouched down to a hole large enough for both of us to gaze through.

"Listen," I whispered back. "We need to check on Antoinette Bazile. Claims to be an American. May or may not be married to our friend, Slim-Jim. Whose name is really Toussaint Leautaud."

"Now where have I heard that name before?"

"From me. I told you about the slave revolt in Haiti. The name of their leader was Toussaint Louverture."

"No relation then, I presume."

"Could be if he's Haitian which is likely judging by his name. Martin Cook is looking into this, as well."

"You're supporting Martin's entire business."

Martin Cook owns a process serving agency in D.C. His staff of ten act as couriers for law firms and serve subpoenas, summons and complaints. Martin does legwork on databases he has no business poking around in. I use him only as a last resort. This had struck me as a last resort.

"Jon Douglas claims not to know that Ricky hangs out here," I said.

"And you believe him?"

"No."

"You'd better not get involved with him," Bob said.

"I know."

We were watching a small courtyard covered with a thatched roof held up by wooden posts. Painted the same dark red as the porch and decorated with white *vévé*s.

"What's with the signs?" Bob whispered.

"Magical emblems which call forth the spirits."

"What, from wooden posts?"

"No, that's decoration. The real *vevés* are traced on the ground around the middle post in corn flour mixed with ashes. Not easy to do, very intricate. And magical, done by the priest."

"Ah," Bob said.

The post in the middle—the *poteau-mitan*—taller than the corner posts, raised the roof slightly. It was surrounded by what looked like a picnic table of rough-hewn planks. Several drums hung from the palm fronds which formed the roof. The floor in the middle was compacted clay hard enough to dance on.

The moans swelled and turned into cries of ecstacy.

"What's with the moaning? I can't make out anyone," Bob said.

"They're there. On the benches around the peristyle."

"The what?"

"Voudou talk for this kind of covered shed."

The figures moved like shadows in the breeze and the palm fronds above trembled with sudden gusts of wind.

Around the periphery were several rows of wooden benches with immobile figures.

A hush fell over the peristyle

"What's going on?" Bob whispered.

"You'll see in a minute," I said. "You're about to experience some amazing voudou."

Out of the shadows came a tall, slender man, buck-naked except for a skimpy, loose-hanging loincloth which did nothing to disguise him. He lifted his arms and carefully sprinkled himself with liquid from a spray bottle. From the table around the middle post he grabbed a white towel and dried himself.

"Some shower," Bob mumbled.

"Purification."

"What's going on now, you who seem to know so much?"

"He's the *Houngan* and he may be in his birthday suit but he looks a lot like Slim-Jim Toussaint," I said.

"Yeah, that's him."

"He has just prepared himself for a sacrifice," I said.

"Oh, Jeez."

"He's going to test that poor white chicken over there. If the chicken eats the grain she's done for."

"And if not?"

"Then another hapless chick is chosen."

"I'm rooting for this one," Bob said.

Toussaint reeled around the center post. His limbs were stiff. He threw his head back. His feet beat a tap along with the intensified drumming. He circled around the white chicken which sealed its own fate by gobbling up grain from the ground.

It happened swiftly. He grabbed the chick by its legs and swung it around his head four times. He zig-zagged around the floor like a drunken sailor.

"Oh, God, is this legal?" Bob moaned and I'll admit I almost lost it myself because I knew what was coming.

The end for the chicken was brutal.

Toussaint stretched out its neck and sank his teeth deep into it. Blood squirted into his face and onto the ground. He struggled with the wreathing body. Then he pulled the chicken's head off with a quick maneuver involving both hands.

When it was over he plucked a few feathers off the breast of the chicken and stuck them onto the center pole with smears of blood.

I turned to Bob and saw he might have missed the last actions. His head was turned and he looked quite white in the face.

The drummers in the corner kept up the beats for a while longer. There were three drums of varying sizes each one being beaten in a different way.

One was struck with the hand by a guy in dreadlocks.

The second was held firmly in place between the legs of a seated guy in a head-scarf. He drummed rapidly.

The third drum was struck with two sticks, monotonously and insistently. The drummer handed the sticks to a different man who applied them less expertly and stopped after a few beats. The drummer took back his sticks.

The amateur drummer wiped his face on his sleeve and walked along the back of the benches towards the exit.

His gait made me look closer.

Chapter 18

"Bob. See the guy at the back. Does he look white to you?"

"Sure does." Bob said and turned on his heel. I pulled my feet out of the soggy ground and followed him towards the front of the building. We got to the street almost at the same time and stayed in the shadows waiting for Ricky to appear. And waited. But no one came out the front door.

"Around the corner," Bob said and we ran.

A car engine turned over in the alley followed by the squeal of tires.

"There he goes," Bob shouted.

We reached Bob's rental car just as the car—an old Ford—made a U-turn in the street.

"Damn," Bob shouted. "Why didn't we catch him inside. Now we have to chase him and he'll get nervous. Doesn't know who we are."

We left the French Quarter without picking up much speed. Ricky wasn't in any apparent hurry. Bob stayed well behind and let several other cars in between before turning on his lights.

"We're going on to the highway," I said. "Maybe he's moved across the Mississippi River and that's why we haven't found him."

"Except he's been hanging out in the French Quarter in several bars alone. It's puzzling. If he doesn't want to be found why has he been so visible?"

The Ford picked up speed on Route 90 and we were soon on the bridge across the river and onto the Westbank Expressway. At Westwego Ricky suddenly swung into the outside lane and disappeared from sight at an exit where an all but invisible sign announced the entrance to a Bayou Swamp Reserve.

Bob changed lanes but narrowly missed the exit. He swore loud and long, swerved into the breakdown lane and backed up against traffic, lights flashing. A stream of cars passed us tooting their horns. Bob waited until the coast was clear and managed to exit. When we got to the end of the ramp there were two choices, to the left or to the right.

"Left," I shouted and pointed down the road to the tail-lights from a single car. Bob and I have done this kind of driving together countless times in the Washington area with either one of us steering and the other reconnoitering. It felt like the good old days.

"Gotcha," Bob said and careened too close to the Ford.

Ricky, alerted, picked up speed and disappeared down a dirt road and across a narrow bridge.

"We're losing him."

"Watch me," Bob said and leaned on the gas.

"Stop."

Bob switched to the brakes just in time.

Ricky had left his car blocking the end of the bridge. We saw him slam the door and run down a low embankment to a trail where he disappeared.

"Damn," Bob shouted.

We stumbled out of the car and ran. The trail took us down to a wooden cabin and a pier.

The small motor boat was several lengths out in the water making an infernal racket. No one onboard could have heard Bob shouting nor probably seen him in the pitch dark night.

We careened to the end of the pier and stopped short.

"There's a second boat," Bob shouted. "Let's go."

I engage in sailsports out of Annapolis and could probably have jimmied the engine and got us going. But too late for that. A shadow rose up from the bottom of the boat, the engine started with another infernal rumble and it took off into the dark.

"We're sunk," Bob said.

"Yes, we are."

We went back to Ricky's Ford.

"You get the licence plate," I said. "I'll see what's inside the car."

The doors were unlocked, the key was still in the ignition. Probably wouldn't have happened if he hadn't been in such a hurry.

"Nothing in the glove compartment."

"Louisiana licence plate," Bob said.

"Will you have it traced or shall I?" I said.

"I'll do it."

"Nothing," I said. "Nothing on the floor, nothing in the pockets."

"I'm checking the trunk," Bob said.

The duffelbag was green and contained one pair of jeans. Levi's. Two white t-shirts without logos. Two pairs of white socks and a pair of never used Reeboks.

"Is this Ricky's size?" I pulled out the jeans. Also brand-new.

"He's shorter than I am."

Bob held up the jeans and we looked at them in the light from the car. They looked short.

"Are Reeboks his style?"

"Swears by them."

"What are you doing?" I said.

"I'm leaving a note for Ricky. He didn't realize who we were."

"Okay."

Chapter 19

The Bayou, August 12, 2005

"The wife might recognize him," he said. "I don't."

Bob took back Ricky's picture. It was five in the morning and we were near the cabin by the pier where we'd lost Ricky. Speaking to the captain of a small ferry boat.

His face was the color of tanned leather, deeply lined. He was long-jawed and big-boned with hands like shovels. His bushy eyebrows straggled above his bright blue eyes. He looked older than he probably was.

"You're out early," he said. "What's your business?"

Bob took out his PI licence.

"I'm a private investigator. Formerly FBI." And he produced his former FBI identification. The one he's technically not supposed to use.

"And who are you, Miss?" the captain said to me.

"Jamie Prescott. Private Investigator," I said and showed him my D.C. licence. The one I renew faithfully every year never mind the travel business.

The captain smiled with crooked teeth.

"The name's Brogan. They call me Cap'n Pete."

He stuck out his hand and crunched my fingers to pieces.

"Does your wife get up early, too?" I said.

"On her feet by four."

"We'd like to show her the picture. Do you live in the cabin up there?" I pointed.

Cap'n Pete laughed.

"No, no, we live out a ways in the bayou. Forty minutes."

"Could you take us there now?"

"Supposin' I could."

"We'd like to hire you for the day," I said.

"I got a group at eleven. Can't miss that."

"We'll be back by then. We appreciate it, Cap'n Pete."

"You go ahead an' call me Pete."

"Pete it is," I said. "Pete, did you see an old Ford blocking the bridge this morning?"

"No, ma'am."

"Didn't think so," Bob said.

The ferry boat sat high in the shallow water. Pete stood at the back behind the wheel and Bob and I sat on one of the wooden benches which ran the length of the boat. Meant for about forty tourists.

"At least we know that Ricky got the message you left in his car," I said to Bob.

"Sure."

The boat swung around slowly and set out towards true bayou country. We were the only traffic on the water.

"Didn't know that people actually live out there," I shouted above the engine.

"Yes'm, since 1765. We are Cajuns and proud of it. We're descended from the French Acadians expelled from Nova Scotia by the British. We still speak the French tongue. We're farmers and fishermen."

"It was a long way from there to here," I said.

"Took'm thirty years. They roamed around as displaced persons. Only state would take'm was Louisiana."

"And the Creoles?"

"Means Europeans born in the colonies. From the Spanish *criollo.*"

We were steering into a maze of twisting waterways in some places so narrow that we could touch the trees on the banks. Then suddenly into a wider stretch. Bald cypress trees stood in water with their gnarled, cone-shaped knees jutting up around their trunks.

"Out-growths from their submerged roots," Pete said before we could ask. "Seems the trees need some relief from all the water they're standing in."

"Spanish moss," I said instead. A ghostly blanket of pale green dangled from the willows towards the swamp water.

"It's not moss at all," Pete said. "Not parasitic like vines which strangle their hosts. These are air plants without roots. They get their nutrition from dust particles and the moist air. Epiphytic."

"Epiphytic," Bob said.

"The French called it *barbe espagnole* and the Spanish responded with *peluca francesa* but the French expression, modified, carried the day."

Pete looked pleased at the thought.

"The moss pickers would set out in their flat barges," he said. "They'd collect the moss with long poles or climb up the trees and throw it straight down into the boat. Then came the curing in the sun over several months. And then it was hung up to dry and bound into bales ready to ship on."

"What for?" Bob said.

"Ah. In the olden days they used it for stuffing mattresses. Very convenient. No bugs ever lived in Spanish moss. On the plantations you'll see the big old beds have six foot rolling pins resting at the ends. Used to be that the servants must roll the mattresses every day to flatten out the lumps."

"Hah," Bob said.

"All gone with the wind. Now we sleep on foam rubber." Pete's eyes twinkled but not without nostalgia.

Bob and I stood at the side of the boat staring into the water. The air was humid and warming up, intensifying the purples and blues and yellows of the water hyacinths that blanketed the water.

"Beautiful," I said and Pete heard me.

"Beautiful but deadly," he said.

"What do you mean? Are they poisonous?"

"Not to you and me. But they spread like wildfire. They clog the waterways. They choke off other vegetation. And they cut off the sunlight needed for aquatic life."

"Wow. How did they get here?"

"By mistake. Brought from Japan for the International Cotton Exposition in New Orleans in 1884. A flower was given to each visitor and soon fountains and fish ponds and, then, the waterways and bayous were filled with hyacinths. Imagine about a million plants in an acre of water."

"Why not get rid of them?"

"Why not?" Pete laughed. And laughed again. He was used to tourists.

"For over a hundred years they've tried. They first came in with pitchforks. They've tried chewing them into pulp. Then dynamite. Then fire. Then arsenic. Not a good idea that last one."

"And I thought they looked so beautiful," I said.

"They are that," Pete said.

"Crocodile," Bob shouted.

Pete laughed. Tourists are a riot.

"Alligator," he said.

"I knew that," Bob said.

"Square snouts. Crocs have pointy noses."

"I did not know that."

"Oldest creatures around. Outlived the dinosaurs. Survived the ice age thirteen thousand years ago."

"That would account for the wrinkles," Bob said.

Cap'n Pete didn't laugh.

"Cute over-bite, though," Bob said.

Cap'n Pete laughed.

Chapter 20

"Coo-eee, Coo-eee."

Pete slowed down the boat and cut the engine.

The waters pulsed slowly around us, the silence was absolute. Only a still breeze moved the tops of trees and trembled through shrouds of dusty-green moss. A maze of small waterways went nowhere and everywhere. Patches of sunlight cast shadows on the surface. The water was covered from bank to bank with green scum.

"That's not scum," Pete, the mind-reader, said. "That's duckweed. Smallest flowers in the world."

Banjo frogs called from afar rattling their vocal cords like loose banjo strings. An egret stood poised, its neck a graceful *S,* its egg-shaped body supported by two stick legs, its pointy beak at the ready to snap up a prey.

"Coo-eee, Coo-eee," Pete called and two tree logs separated from the bank and glided towards us, their snouts barely above water.

They were nine feet long with bulging eyes and warty skin.

"Good teeth," Bob said. "Nasty fellows."

"Not at all." Pete's face set into grimness. "Peaceful. Non-aggressive. We control their numbers so there's plenty of natural food. Don't need to eat tourists. Not like Florida. Here you can swim with them. Won't bother you."

"Not putting it to the test," Bob said.

"Chicken," I said.

"They won't eat chickens, either," Cap'n Pete said.

Heaven save me from people lacking a sense of humor. It's such heavy going.

"And the Florida alligators do?" I couldn't help myself. Should've left it alone.

"That's because they don't control the numbers," Pete said letting the boat idle. "When there's a lack of natural food the gators get aggressive and go after chickens and even babies."

Bob and I stared at the foot-long rows of sharp teeth snapping around the giant marshmallows Pete tossed into the water. The gators waited in place hoping for more. When the sweets stopped coming they curved their tails and returned to the bank as tree logs.

Pete got us going again and we entered a wide waterway.

"About Doc Winnipeg," I said to Bob. "He's not a podiatrist."

"Fast work. He's legit?"

"He's an ophthalmologist."

"No!"

"Yes. And his real name is Hubert Huffnagel."

"No!"

"Yes."

"What did he do?"

"Seems he cheated Medicare out of hundreds of thousands. Had a lot of fake patients. Got caught, lost his licence, plea-bargained, got probation, made restitution, did community service, changed his name, moved from Ohio to Louisiana."

"What do you think?" Bob looked amused.

"Let's not worry about him."

"And his non-profit organization?"

"Still checking."

"You using Martin Cook?"

"Fastest gun in the east."

"Did you have him check on the title to the house Ricky is renting?"

"I did."

"Well?"

"He couldn't find the records."

"Why not? It's public."

"That's exactly what *I* said."

"And?" Bob said.

"He'll get back to me on that one, too."

"Over there," Pete said and pointed.

A pier sitting on thin wooden poles jutted into the water. A small motor boat was tied to the pier.

We putt-putted in a wide circle. Pete jumped ashore, secured the ferry boat, put down a narrow gangplank and invited us to walk it. He shouted something that sounded suspiciously like his alligator coo-eee.

"Now the wife knows I'm home," he said.

If I didn't know this was his wife I'd have thought she was his sister. Same long face. Same strong forehead and forbidding nose. Black eyebrows. Her body was a solid piece of sturdiness. Her gray hair was gathered with a red rubber band and curled down her back.

The hand she offered me was broad and calloused. Reluctantly, I let her squeeze the one Pete had recently bruised.

"Mother," Pete said. "These here folks want to ask you something."

"Come in."

"Folks, this here is the wife, Yvette."

We all said nice to meet you and Yvette said "will you have some coffee?"

"Thank you, ma'am," Bob said and I thought longingly of the Café Du Monde café-au-lait.

The cabin—with an outhouse at the back—sat high on a bank in the shade of the tall cypresses. It had two small rooms with the combined living area and kitchen in front. There was a pervasive smell of woodstove. The coffee came in a blue enameled pot served in enameled mugs.

She sat at the table and watched us stir in the brown sugar. No milk. I sipped. The coffee was undrinkable. I stirred in three more spoonfuls of sugar. It didn't help. I abandoned the mug discreetly.

The wife folded her hands in her lap and said nothing. She hadn't cracked a smile since we arrived. Looked as if she swam with alligators.

"Ma'am," Bob said. He's not usually rattled but her steady stare made his voice rasp. "We won't take up much of your time. Just need to know if you recognize this photograph."

He held it out to her but she didn't look at it. She looked at Bob and then she looked at me.

"How do you know these folks?" she said and turned to Pete. "You seen them before?"

"No. No, I haven't," Pete said. "But look at their papers. They're detectives from Washington."

We quickly produced our credentials and she looked at them carefully. Then she picked up the photograph from the table and took a good look.

"Did he do something wrong?" she said.

"No, not at all," Bob said. "He's a friend of mine and he seems to have disappeared. Do you recognize him?"

"I do."

Chapter 21

"He came a week ago when Pete was away shrimping."

"How did he find you," I said.

"Everyone knows they can stop here and buy a hot meal. Catfish 'n gumbo. Mostly. And coffee."

"What was he doing out here?"

"A journalist, he says."

"Doing what?" Bob said.

"Wanting to write about bayou country."

"Did he come alone?" I said.

"Yes, ma'am."

"In a small motor boat?"

"Yes, ma'am."

It was like pulling teeth.

"Did he say where he was staying?"

"In N'awlins."

"Did he say where he was going?"

"As he said, into the bayou. He should have gone with someone. Easy to get lost. Told him so."

"What did he say?" I said.

"Laughed a bit."

"But he continued into the bayou?"

"A ways."

"So you know where he went?"

"No."

"Your best guess?"

"As good as anyone's."

Bob got up from the table. And so did I. End of this line. Better get going.

"One more thing," Bob said. "Did you notice boat traffic out here late last night?"

Yvette looked at him, thinking.

"We did," she said. "Not often we have boats in the middle of the night. There were two."

"Do you have any idea where they might have gone?"

"How could we?"

"I mean," I said. "Are there any other places like yours out here?"

"Not near here. The boats came back later. That's all we know."

Yvette got up and crossed her arms above her stomach. Or somewhere near. She looked at Pete who got up in a hurry. Guess he didn't swim with alligators after all.

"We'll be off, then," Pete said and Bob and I trooped out behind him. Yvette scrambled with the enameled mugs as the wooden door closed.

A thick, low mist was settling around the edges of the banks spreading a green haze across the bayou. Not a ripple on the water. Not a stir through the trees. Pete looked up and sniffed the air on our way down the small pier to the ferry boat.

"Storm coming along," he said. "Won't give us much time. Hop in."

We did and stood near Pete as he started up the engine.

"The water doesn't seem to be flowing at all," I said and waited for Pete's response. It wasn't long in coming.

"It's deceptive. The water may flow east all day at a very slow pace. In the evening it reverses course and flows west. Bayous come and go so fast that no one bothers to map them anymore. It's all connected to the tides of the Gulf. Very deceptive. When a hurricane comes in from the sea the waters here get flooded with salt water."

"That can't be good," I said.

"No, ma'am. But that's not all. Goes back a long time. The oil companies violated the wetlands. They have a lot to answer for. They built canals for navigation which eroded the soil. That allowed salt water to enter the marshes, the salinity killed the plants whose roots held the soil in place. And we're losing wetland every second of the day and night."

Pete suddenly looked self-conscious at his own eloquence.

"Heavy rainfalls can cause flooding all by themselves," he said. "Looks as if we're in for something in a couple of hours."

Pete swung the boat in a wide circle. But instead of returning to our point of origin he steered it across the water. We entered a narrow channel hidden by floating branches below and mossy offshoots above. It was just wide enough for the boat to squeeze through. Purple water hyacinths blanketed the surface. You could touch the vegetation on the banks on both sides.

"Mother wouldn't like this," Pete said and slowed the boat to a crawl. "The bottom fills up with silt, a boat could get stuck. But it's a shortcut. We'll be out of it soon enough. Somethin' I want to look at."

We didn't come out of it soon, it was more like fifteen minutes. The boat slithered forward cautiously, rocking a bit when it hit something on the bottom. Pete held it steady by pushing it off the side of the bank with a pole. The moss dangled and a racoon on the bank looked up unconcerned and continued battling with a tree branch.

"Alligators," Bob exclaimed when a couple of logs tumbled off the bank and disappeared underwater. The underground foliage rustled and a flock of birds complained and flew to the top of a tree.

"Sure 'nuff," Pete said and looked at Bob with a wicked twinkle. "Keep your hands inside the boat."

We burst out from the dark tunnel into sunlight and entered a horse-shoe enclosure. Pete circled out and around and slowly approached a pier partly hidden by broken branches.

He secured the boat, put down the gangplank, and helped us up on the pier.

"Used to be that ole Jim Villiers lived in the cabin up there. No one lives there now. Heard some fishermen have used it on and off."

The fog hung close to the water's surface and curled up around our feet. A sudden windburst ripped through the tree-tops. We saw it at the same time. Bob swore under his breath and I held mine.

A small motorboat lay upside down close to the bank, oil still seeping from out under.

Chapter 22

"Pull," Bob shouted.

"I'm pulling."

"Push," Pete said and hooked his pole around the railing. "Now."

The motorboat turned with a splash.

"Have you seen it before?" I asked.

"Can't say that I have," Pete said. "It's not from around here."

"But you knew it might be here?"

"Not right here. And not upside down. But not too far off."

"How come?"

"Mother was mistaken," Pete said. "Only one boat returned last night."

"I'm going in," I said.

"Here, put on Mother's boots," Pete said.

He held my hand at arm's length and eased me into the boat. Everything was dripping water and several inches of silt covered the inside. I moved carefully to the small cockpit. Whatever had been there had dropped out when the boat was overturned. There were no clues as to ownership or to former occupants.

Pete hauled me back up.

"Nothing there," I said. "Let's go up to the cabin."

We walked along the narrow pier. Every other plank had disappeared and some of the rest were about to fall out. At the bank we ended up in a foot of water and I heard Bob grunting behind me.

We waded through the brush and sloshed up the bank to the cabin. The silence was humming with tiny noises from insects and frogs and God knew what else. A black and white-speckled spider sat motionless on a green leaf.

The cabin was no more than a shack. Its gray planks had large gaps and the whole thing looked about to collapse. Inside we found a rusty kerosene stove on a wooden counter, a pallet with a grubby blanket, a pair of rubber boots and an old fishing rod.

"Let's have a quick look-see," Bob said.

He kicked at the rubber boots. Nothing came out.

I lifted the blanket.

"Nothing here."

"Let's go," Pete said and held the door open.

We had taken only a few steps outside the cabin when Pete grabbed my arm and pushed Bob behind him.

"Watch out," he said. "Cottonmouth."

The path was narrow with low bushes and tall grasses on either side. Nowhere to sidestep the snake.

The triangular black and yellow head reared up from the ground in front of us. The body—with dark yellow crossbands—was curled up like a rope. It's open mouth was pink as cotton candy, the tongue shot out, and the fangs dripped. It was ready. It all happened very fast. The head moved back, darted forward, and the fangs dug into Pete's boot.

Bob and I jumped back into the shack, Pete whacked at the snake with his pole, and we all shouted gibberish. It took five whacks before the cottonmouth lost its grip, dropped away, and slithered back into the underbrush.

"Devil of a thing," Pete said.

He sank down on one knee and took off his boot.

"Didn't penetrate," he said.

"Oh, God," I said.

"It happens," Pete said. "Thing is to have sturdy boots."

"And look what *we're* wearing," I said. My shoes weren't exactly Manolo Blahniks but close enough and Bob had on Docksers.

"Let's go," Bob said. "And let's take the boat."

Pete got a rope attached and the small motor boat floated behind us.

"Can we find out who owns it?" Bob asked.

"Should be able to," Pete said. "Supposed to have the Hull Identification Number attached. Except I don't see it."

"Owners can't be traced then?"

"No, sir."

"Hell," Bob said.

"Yes."

"Means it was stolen?"

"Stands to reason," Pete said.

We were back in the ferry boat and Pete tossed us some rough socks big enough for elephant feet.

"Mother knits," Pete said. "They'll do until we can get you to shore and dry your shoes."

Bob and I shivered, put on the socks, and huddled close to Pete in the small cockpit.

The sky was now swollen with heavy clouds. They were an ominous color of black and yellow and were whipped along by strong winds. There was a sound of thunder from afar. A few raindrops came down, then several, then a torrent. The rain drummed on the roof of the cockpit and ran down the length of the boat.

The water churned with the wind. Branches, leaves, and moss hurtled through the air. A large tree trunk shot past the boat and it wasn't an alligator. A snapping turtle scrambled up the bank.

"No point in leaving," Pete said. "We're in a horseshoe. Unless the water rises we're okay."

"And if it does?" I said.

"We'll wait for it to recede."

"How long could that take?"

"Hours."

"Oh, God."

We huddled in silence while the wind screamed through the treetops. Pete stood at the railing, his head up, listening. Once in a while he nodded as if he'd gotten a good piece of news from upstairs. The wind blew way above our horseshoe inlet and disappeared beyond the trees.

The storm was gone as swiftly as it had arrived.

We sat a few more minutes without speaking until Pete turned and smiled. His eyes were very blue but his teeth hadn't seen a dentist in years.

"That's it," he said.

Then he turned and leaned back over the side of the boat. He grabbed his pole and poked at something. He grunted and raised a hand.

Bob and I went to the railing.

The water hyacinths covered the bayou like a quilt of bright colors with sporadic clearings where branches and dead tree logs collided and fought for space. The boat had created a gap in the blanket of flowers and we stared in silence.

The body was floating face down in the water.

Chapter 23

"Over here."

"Don't push."

"He's floating away."

"Get the hook into his jacket."

"It keeps slipping off."

Cap'n Pete grabbed my arm with a fistful of callouses.

"I'll hold you," he said and pushed me towards the railing.

"What, and hang me overboard?"

It's not that I'm afraid of heights. Or afraid of dangling head first over the side of a boat. It wasn't that I didn't trust Pete to hold me. It was more like 'why am I always the first choice.'

"Bob's too heavy for us to hold," Pete said. "But he and I can easily hold *you*. Only way we can get'im before 'e floats away. Wind's picking up. Squalls rising."

"Fine," I said and stepped out of my elephant socks. "But don't let go."

I climbed up on the rail—a good five feet above the water's surface—and straddled the wide rim. I leaned over and looked down. The body was slamming against the side. Strong waves pushed and pulled. It was only a matter of minutes before we lost him.

"Okay, grab her," Pete shouted and I felt his grip on my right ankle. "Grab her other leg."

"Okay, I got her." Bob grabbed with both hands.

I swung over the rail head first and fell like a sack of potatoes. Tore off the skin of my knuckles, too. The planks felt like sandpaper and rasped as my body slammed against the side.

My left leg swung loose from Bob's grip. My face hit the water. Pete's hand slipped from my ankle.

I sank down head first.

The water was murky. I swallowed some and prepared to swim with alligators. I'm not normally chicken, but still. In the meantime I was caught in the tough roots from water hyacinths. They crawled around my arms like so many octopus tentacles.

I let out my breath in very small bubbles and held it when I had no more air left. I somersaulted and got my head above water just as stars formed behind my closed eyelids.

My head bumped into Ricky's soft body. I embraced his middle and kicked my legs. The body and I had floated ten feet away by the time I sighted the boat.

I turned on my back and swam.

Bob and Pete were safely aboard hanging over the side, mouths agape. I couldn't hear a thing. Whatever they shouted got carried away on strong gusts of wind and by the sloshing of water over my head.

The body turned in my arms. I tightened my hold on the tweed jacket. It was slippery to the touch. The jacket rode up from the hips to the waist and to the chest.

I lost my grip.

I sensed the alligators and saw their shadows out of the corner of my eye. They floated past me without making even the smallest splash in the water. I opened my mouth to scream and muddy water rushed in. I had three seconds in which to make a decision. Couldn't for the life of me recall what to do during a close encounter with alligators. Stay immobile? Leave stealthily? Believe Pete? In the end, my panic button propelled me into fleeing. I spat out water, latched onto the body one more time, turned it around and kicked us back the now twenty some feet to the boat. The alligators floated away and disappeared.

The body became heavier by the minute, my own clothes were soaked and weighed me down. I swam on my back to preserve my strength and to keep the flood water out of my face. I turned the body and stuck my arms under its armpits. Then I kicked a few more times until I reached the boat.

"Hold on," Pete shouted and the next thing I knew he had dropped into the water next to me. He grabbed the body with one hand and helped me up with the other. Bob did the rest. My arms were wrenched nearly out of their sockets, my hands got another good scraping, and I landed on my knees on the deck.

"Hey, help me here," Bob screamed and I crawled back to the rail. "Pete's tying a rope around the body."

Bob had the end of the rope wrapped around his arms and hung over the rail, both feet about to leave the deck. I hung on to Bob. The body swung in the air while we pulled and Pete pushed. First came the head, then the torso, and a moment later the body rested across the rail on its stomach. Water poured out of the mouth.

We pulled one last time and the body fell on the deck.

We threw the rope back to Pete and he climbed aboard. Bob was on his knees, Pete lay on his side, and I had sat down square on my butt.

The body lay face down with water oozing slowly along the planks from the soggy clothing.

Bob reached over and turned the body on its back.

"Hell's bells," he said.

Chapter 24

"It's Brad Sorensen."

"What do you mean?"

"That's Brad Sorensen. Special Agent. FBI."

"That's not Ricky Wilson?"

"No."

"You sure?"

"Sure's hell."

"You mean we've been tracking the wrong guy all along?" I said.

"Sure's hell."

"Could you say something more constructive?"

"Don't know. Give me a minute. Can't think." Bob's face was white.

"Okay, let me help," I said. "How about we're one degree removed from Ricky."

"Or that we've stumbled down the wrong alley."

"One or the other."

Pete got up, went to the cockpit, and started up the boat. He swung it around and set out towards the wide opening of the horse-shoe inlet. The small motor boat bumped up and down on the waves behind us but the rope held. Apparently we were taking the long way around.

"Bottom may have shifted in the narrow canal we came from. Waves churn up the water, deposit silt. Can't risk it," Pete said.

"We're going back to shore," Bob said.

"You want me to contact police beforehand? Got the radio," Pete said.

"We'll wait. I'll call when we arrive. How long will it take?"

"Fifty minutes."

"You got a tarp we can wrap him in?"

"Under the seat behind me."

We hauled it out and Bob dragged it across to the body and covered it up. Then he and I sat down on the floor behind Pete and I began to shiver in my wet clothes. Pete took off his shirt and pants and put on a black cape.

"Here," he said. "I've got some extra pants and a sweat-shirt in the duffel over there. We'll turn around while you change."

"I'm too frozen to be modest," I said and peeled off everything.

The pants were gargantuan, the sweat shirt humongous.

"Belong to the wife," Pete said. "Should fit you. There's a pair of boots somewheres. Root around."

I may be tall but my feet are a size eight. The boots were a twelve so I put on Mother's elephant socks to fill them up. I was all set.

"My God, you look awful," Bob said.

"Thank you."

"No, I mean you're blue in the face."

"Wrap yourself in this," Pete said and tossed me a stiff gray army blanket.

The boat was going at full speed, the banks with the dangling moss flew past us in a haze, the body under the tarp still oozed water on the deck, and Bob and I huddled at the back of the cockpit to get out of the wind.

"Okay, shoot," I said. "What's going on? Who's Brad Sorensen?"

"He is—he was—with the Special Investigations Unit. They are assigned to covert operations."

"So he came here to look for Ricky as a roving reporter for a non-existent newspaper?"

"Or, better still, as a free-lance journalist," Bob said.

"Yes, that would give him the utmost flexibility."

"All he needed was a press pass."

"And to look like an insurance salesman," I said and thought of the bartender at the Monteleone.

"Right," Bob said and got up. "Sit tight. I'm going to search his pockets."

I helped him pull off the tarp. The body couldn't have been in the water more than twelve hours. There was some bloating but Bob went through the inner and outer pockets in Brad's jacket, then of his pants. He came up with some loose change but no wallet. In the back pants pocket there was a piece of crumpled paper. The water had removed all trace of writing. We put the tarp back and returned to the cockpit.

"Didn't think so," Bob said. "But there might have been something."

"Yeah," I said. "And you're sure it's Brad Sorensen?"

"I'm telling you it's Brad. No doubt about it."

"Those photographs of Ricky could just as well apply to Brad Sorensen?"

"There's a resemblance."

"That leaves the question, where's Ricky?" I said.

Pete cut the engine and the ferry boat coasted down the channel. He made a couple of maneuvers until the boat bumped against the pier at the swamp station. The water was churning up again and he got out his pole to hold us steady.

"Here," said Bob the sailor-man and grabbed one end of a rope which lay curled up on the deck. "I'll pull you in."

"No," Pete and I shouted in unison as Bob squeezed out between the gate and the raised gangplank.

The boat veered away on a sudden wave.

Bob hovered in the air a second before he fell between the boat and the pier.

The boat slammed back and Bob screamed.

Chapter 25

"It's broken. My leg is broken."

"Just lie still. The ambulance is on its way."

"Hurts like hell," Bob said.

"You were lucky the pier wasn't a solid slab of cement. You were lucky the boat pushed you under the wooden stilts."

"Yes, I feel lucky."

"What were you thinking?" I said and folded Pete's blanket under his head.

"Got another blanket?" I shouted to Pete and he tossed me one from the boat.

"You must leave Brad's body in the boat," Bob whispered. "Get my cell phone, please."

I got it from his pocket and flipped it open. It gave a pathetic beep and went blank.

"That's a gonner," I said. "Give me the number and I'll call. I take it you don't want 911?"

"Right." Bob didn't look as if he could hold it together much longer. He gave me a number, slowly, while I dialed. I handed him my phone but he trembled too hard to grab it. I held the phone to his ear.

"Bob Makowski here," he said and followed it with something I didn't catch. "I've got Brad Sorensen's body in a ferry boat at the pier at the swamp reserve off of Route 90. Captain's name's Pete Brogan. He'll be watching for you.

And don't hassle him, he knows nothing and had zip to do with this."

Bob listened to the voice at the other end. His face was getting white with the effort.

"Yes, he's dead and no, I can't wait. I'm on my way to the hospital with a broken leg. You take over and be quick about it. And, no, I don't know how it happened. It's your funeral."

"Hang up," Bob said to me and fainted.

I pulled up his pants leg and took a closer look. The shinbone was red and swollen and his foot twisted at an unnatural angle.

"Pete," I shouted. "Bob wants you to stand watch over the body. Someone official will appear soon and remove it."

"Okay." Pete said.

"Here. This is my card with all my possible phone numbers in New Orleans and in Washington. Call me if there's a problem."

"Are the police coming?"

"More like the FBI," I said. "But they will call themselves something else. Not to worry. Perfectly legit."

"Ah," Pete said. "Let me go to the office. I need someone else to take the eleven o'clock tour."

He returned, mission accomplished, just as the tour group arrived and was diverted to a different boat and the ambulance pulled up. Two paramedics showed up on the pier with a stretcher and lifted the white-faced Bob onto it.

"We're taking him to Tulane University emergency room," the driver said to me.

"I'll follow you."

"Take Route 90 across the river, then Route 10 to Tulane Avenue. Can't miss it."

You don't know me, I thought. I who gets lost in parking lots.

"You take care, Miss," Pete shouted when I got in my rental car.

"You, too. And sorry for the trouble."

How inadequate was that but Pete had kept his Cajun composure well.

I lost the ambulance somewhere on the Pontchartrain Expressway and it was another half hour before I parked near the hospital emergency room entrance. They had taken Bob in already and I sat in the waiting room anticipating the news. If I knew anything about Bob, and I know plenty, he'd want to get back to Washington immediately.

Two hours later they wheeled him out and to a room on the third floor, asleep, with his right leg hoisted up by an alarming contraption and his arm hooked up to an IV. They handed me a bag with his soaked clothing and I settled down in a chair to watch over him.

An hour later he woke up and stared at me in confusion.

"Helluva thing," he mumbled.

"You can say that again," I said.

Chapter 26

Washington, August 14, 2005

As I expected, Bob wanted to get back to Washington and check into GWU hospital. The staff at Tulane were palpably glad to be rid of him. He's cantankerous with his limbs intact and took out the embarrassment caused by his own stupidity on everyone. On the first day his leg was x-rayed and the tibia declared fractured. A cast was ordered. On the second day Bob instructed me to pack his bags and get our tickets. We left that afternoon.

We got to the Louis Armstrong airport in a minibus where a nurse installed Bob in the back seat with his leg stretched out. I'd alerted the airline that we needed a wheelchair at the curb and they were there in force. One attendant hoisted Bob out of the vehicle, the other received him into the chair, a third took charge of our bags.

"Pleasure, Ms. Prescott," a fourth said and handed me our boarding cards. How's that for being a travel agent.

We went first class.

"Feeling better already," Bob said.

"Ready to hash over the happenings?" I said.

"Sure. But first I need one of my little pills."

"Pain getting to you?"

"No, I need some sleep. They woke me up every four hours and if they didn't, the one in the bed next to me moaned all night. Get me some water, will you."

Bob slept like a baby and I tossed and turned in my leather seat all the way to Reagan National Airport.

The services resumed at that end. Airline staff appeared with a wheelchair and we were whisked through the arrival hall to an ambulance sent from GWU hospital. The paramedics made room for me in the front seat and the driver—a woman with a capable but stern demeanor—took us across the Potomac River on the Arlington Memorial Bridge, around the gleaming Lincoln Memorial and down 23rd Street.

The royal treatment continued at the hospital. Bob was soon installed in a private room with a view and getting fussed over by doctors and staff. He was wheeled off to be re-examined and returned to his room without the cast and with the news that the fracture had to be repaired surgically.

"They talked about a metal rod and wires." Bob stared at me with a pathetic look in his eyes. "Helluva thing."

"They also said it's routine and that you'll be good as new within a month. The skin wasn't broken and there's no nerve damage."

"All the same," Bob said as the phone beside his bed rang.

"Yes," he said. "Yes, sir."

Bob slid down some on his pillows.

"No, sir," he said and rolled his eyes at me.

"Yes, sir," Bob said again.

The voice ran on and on.

"Absolutely," Bob said. "I read you loud and clear, Sir. Goodbye, sir."

He handed me the receiver and I put it back in place.

"What was that all about?" I said.

"Deputy director. FBI."

"The deputy director himself?"

"It's gone all the way to the top," Bob said.

"What did he say?"

"Very cryptic. Couldn't talk freely on this phone but ordered me to stop interfering in Bureau business. With immediate effect. Reminded me I'm retired with a sizeable pension. Inferred my status could be in jeopardy. Wonder what's going on."

"As I see it, you're not even supposed to wonder."

"Something big must be going down. And I'm permitted to wonder aloud to you. You're going to be my eyes and ears."

"And legs."

"That, too. You realize you'll have to return to New Orleans."

"Yes."

"I'll set you up with someone from the Bureau. Now we really need the inside scoop."

"Okay, let me know when and where."

"How about your house in Bethesda tomorrow night."

"Fine, if you can arrange it on such short notice."

A food tray was wheeled across Bob's bed and he lifted a couple of metal covers. There was mainly white stuff looking like boiled fish and mashed potatoes and then some green stuff that wiggled.

"You've gotta save me here," Bob said and replaced the covers. "Just looking at it gives me the willies."

"How about roll-ups or pizza?"

"Anything with color."

"I'll be right back."

An hour later we'd finished a large pizza with anchovies and extra cheese and a pint of Ben and Jerry's.

"Let's recap what we know and what we surmise," Bob said. "Let me start. Let's assume that Ricky retired from the Bureau, moved to New Orleans, stumbled onto something, and began to investigate we don't know what. He was brought back in by the Bureau."

"Had a drug problem," I said.

"Did not. You sent the vial to the lab?"

"Getting the results on Thursday."

"He disappeared," Bob said. "His apartment was sanitized. The Bureau furnished Brad Sorensen with a press pass and, possibly, with a fictitious name and sent him to New Orleans to track down Ricky."

"Brad made contact with some of Ricky's new friends, got to play the drums—very inexpertly, I might add—at priestess Antoinette's peristyle," I said.

"Our Slim-Jim, Toussaint, was there when Brad took off towards the swamp."

"But didn't follow Brad. We did, thinking he was Ricky."

"And someone was waiting for Brad at the pier. Someone knew where he was going," Bob said.

"And then he was killed."

"Let's tally up the suspects." Bob lifted both hands and counted. "Monique and Doc Winnipeg. Antoinette and Toussaint. Two nameless and faceless assassins. Brandy Gregory, the bank account co-signer with the fake address. And Jon Douglas."

"Jon Douglas? I don't think so."

"What? Because he's hot?"

"No, because I'm a good judge of character."

"Okay, we'll put him on the list of maybe's," Bob said. "Your phone is ringing at the bottom of your bag."

The thing is, no one can tell from calling your cell phone where in the world you are. Sometimes a blessing, at other times confusing.

"Hi, there," Jon said. "I've been trying to call you. Are we having dinner tonight or what?"

"Or what is right," I said. "I'm no longer in New Orleans. Had to return to Washington on some urgent business."

"What kind of business?"

"Oh, work-related."

"When will you be back?"

"I'll let you know. And thanks for calling."

"I'll let you know and thanks for calling? You can do better than that." Jon sounded as if he was laughing and I could suddenly picture his eyes gleaming at me. "How about so sorry and I can't wait to see you again?"

Bob was glaring at me.

"Yes, something like that, too," I said. "Let me get back to you."

"Yeah, he's hot all right," Bob mumbled.

Chapter 27

Bethesda, August 15, 2005

"Topsy, I'm back."

I entered the travel agency through a door in my hallway. My Cape Cod style house in Bethesda is just off Old Georgetown Road a few blocks from Wisconsin Avenue and the Metro. The travel agency occupies the ground floor and a remodeling job has brought about a separate entrance to the second and third floors where I live.

"How lovely is that," Topsy said. "I was about to send out an SOS. Ellie called in sick and I'm at my wits end."

Mrs. Elczbet Gczyckzy—privately called Ellie but never to her face—is our bossy office manager who never misses a day.

"What's wrong?" I said.

"It's not her. It's her sister."

"Didn't know she had a sister."

"Apparently she does. They share a house. And now she's sick and Ellie must take care of her."

"I knew it was too good to be true," I said. "Having a reliable manager. What else is new?"

"The Peru tours are running on schedule. Someone on a Bolivian tour got flown home from La Paz with altitude sickness. The Scandinavian tours are on schedule, one leaving this evening. Five people lost their luggage between Florence and Rome."

"In other words, everything is normal," I said.

"And I trust you remember you're taking the ten de luxe professional women to Paris, Vienna and Budapest on September 10."

"Not to worry. I'll be back from New Orleans in plenty of time. Say by September 1."

"You mean you're going back there?"

"I'm giving it another ten days," I said.

"Fine. Someone by the name of Jon Douglas has called you three times in the last hour. And you're blushing."

"Am not. What did he want?"

"He wants to sleep with you."

"Don't they all. And apart from that?"

"Apart from that he sounded young."

"How can you tell on the phone?"

"I can always tell."

No one I know can be as butt-insky as Topsy. It's been going on since we met in first grade, continued through high school and college, only interrupted by my sojourn in Paris. And did I mention she's the one who sets me up on disastrous blind dates?

"I'm conducting this one without interference," I said.

"Are you referring to me?"

"I'll say just two words. Bob Deluca."

"He was gorgeous. Spoke five languages. Gave great parties at that Potomac mansion of his," Topsy said.

"He's serving seven to ten for tax evasion and perjury."

"That's Washington for you. You date at your peril. I don't consider it entirely my fault."

"Should I laugh or cry?"

"So, you're dating this Jon Douglas?" Topsy said.

"No, I'm not dating him. I've only seen him twice. And he's too young.

"Does *he* know that?"

"Possibly not," I said. "How's Jack?"

I might have said instead "How's your marriage?"

"I can't do it," Topsy said. "Jack's moving out for the last and final time. And I don't want to discuss it."

"Come upstairs for lunch," I said.

Travel agenting may be a dying occupation for some what with ticketless airlines and internet tour companies. But we've found a profitable niche with exclusive tours for small groups. We follow in the footsteps of literary greats in the capitals of Europe. Enjoy gourmet cooking at wine castles in France. Sail in the wake of the Vikings in Scandinavia, and join archeological digs in South America. We keep three agents, plus Ellie, the manager, and Harold, the gofer, busy year round. Topsy takes some of the tours, we hire guides overseas, and I space my investigative work to fit.

"Fine, I'm on my way," Topsy said.

My living room, dining room, den and kitchen are on the second floor, my three bedrooms on the third. Two and a half baths. And a balcony at the back overlooking some shady trees. I've got some good pieces of antique furniture and a collection of Haitian paintings. I have some fine silver, crystal, and porcelain which I like to pull out when entertaining.

Bob had arranged for his buddy to come by my house at eight. Just after dark. Guess he didn't want to be recognized which he might easily be since Bethesda has turned into Yuppie paradise. New shops, new restaurants and new apartment buildings sprout everywhere.

I replaced the battery in my tape recorder—the one I keep in the drawer of the sideboard—and put in a new tape. I don't tell Bob everything but his buddy would be confiding in me for the record. Legal or not. I re-arranged the chairs and put a tray with drinks on the sideboard.

"Hello," Topsy said and stuck her head in the door. "Here, I sent Harold out for a salad, some cheese, and a baguette. How's that? Got anything to drink?"

"Like Chardonnay?"

"That'll do."

"I guess you want to hear all about it?" I said.

"Shoot."

"Okay. I told you about Toussaint and Antoinette."

"The voudou couple."

"He purified himself and wrung the neck of a chicken and she's a priestess."

"Why is it that you get to have all the fun?" Topsy said.

"Ricky Wilson played the drums at their house but has disappeared. Brad Sorensen tried to play the drums but couldn't."

"Who's Brad Sorensen?"

"Another of Bob Makowski's old buddies from the Bureau. We found him floating in the bayou. Dead."

Topsy put her glass down hard and opened her eyes wide.

"How did it happen?" she said.

"He left Antoinette's house in a hurry. No one followed him from there except for Bob and I. We thought he was Ricky. We got to a swamp area across the river where Brad obstructed a small bridge with his car. Before we could get past it he'd jumped in a motorboat and disappeared."

"What did you do?"

"Wanted to hijack the only other boat there. But someone was in it and took off after Brad."

"When did you find him?" Topsy said.

"The next day. Swimming with alligators," I said and told her about Cap'n Pete Brogan, his severely intimidating wife, our tour around the bayou, finding the overturned boat and, finally, spotting Brad's body and bringing him to shore.

"And Bob had to play the hero and break his leg. What was he thinking?" Topsy said.

"No idea," I said. "Spur of the moment stupidity."

"And this Cap'n Pete led you straight to the place where you found Brad?"

"He'd heard two boats coming but only one returning, he said. The distance hadn't been that far. That's why he thought they might have gone to the deserted cabin. And he was right," I said. "It did strike me as a bit pat at the time."

"Well, I guess he couldn't have had anything to do with it if he helped you find Brad," Topsy said.

"Looks that way," I said.

"And Jon Douglas?" Topsy said. "How does he fit in? Apart from being a sexy saxophonist."

"He's been in the middle of it all from the beginning. He knows Ricky. Claims he was told not to reveal Ricky's whereabouts. Knows everyone. Plays at Queen Monique's *Blues Grotto*."

"And you think he's concealing something?"

"I'm pretty sure," I said. "I intend to find out what it is. But enough about me. What's going on with you?"

"Short story," Topsy said. "Jack has moved out and in six months I'll be single after twenty-three years of marriage."

She sounded upbeat but her face told a different story.

"It's all right for you," she said in a smaller voice. "You *want* to be single. But *I* want to be married. In Washington, if you're not married you're nothing. Present company excepted."

"Thanks, I think."

"You know what I mean."

"Sort of," I said.

"I can't go to the movies by myself. I can't go to a restaurant for dinner by myself. I can't sit home by myself."

"Of course you can, Topsy. I do it all the time. It's liberating," I said.

"Of course I *can*. The thing is, I don't *want* to. And who do you think will be invited to dinner with our former friends, the still married couples. Jack, of course. Always room for a single attractive man. The women won't want me there because I might steal their husbands. And the men will call me secretly thinking I'm an easy mark now that I'm lonely."

"You'll be alone, not lonely."

"I will be lonely. I'm already lonely." Topsy was drinking too much wine.

"Fine," I said. "If you promise not to reciprocate I'll fix you up with some fabulous blind dates."

"You know of any?"

Martin Cook came to mind. He's forty-five, five-six, dark eyed and quite handsome. Topsy is forty-two, five-three, olive eyed and beautiful.

"I have a definite prospect," I said.

"And your mother," Topsy said and polished off the rest of the Chardonnay. "Still roaming around Europe in search of antiques?"

"Medieval churches," I said. "And it's a study tour."

"She's been gone seven months."

"Deserved a sabbatical."

"Didn't know lawyers got to have those."

"Okay, she's taking a year off," I said.

"And she's booked on our professional women's tour."

"She'll be joining us in Paris."

"Except I can't confirm. She didn't leave an address."

"American Express in Paris. Send everything there."

My mother, Ellen Prescott, who doesn't wait for anyone when planning her life. She went to law school at the age of fifty after my father—who was twenty years her senior—died. She's a partner in a small law firm. She tells me she comes from Viking stock in Sweden and says I've inherited some of their stoic traits. She claims it's a compliment.

We finished the last of the salad, had coffee, and I stuck the couple of plates, glasses, and utensils in the dishwasher.

"What are you going to do next?" Topsy said.

"I'm waiting for one of Bob's contacts to tell me all about Ricky Wilson."

Chapter 28

He was a little weasel of a man with furtive eyes and a chin-enhancing goatee. How could Bob think I'd trust him?

"Have a seat," I said and pointed to one of the chairs next to the sideboard. "What's your name?"

"Call me Dick."

"Okay."

He walked around nervously and looked out the window before he sat down in the sofa. He loosened his tie. Yellow with a Las Vegas showgirl.

"What will you drink?" I said. "I got everything within reason."

"You got coffee?"

"Sure, but it'll take a little longer."

"That's fine. Plenty of time."

I walked across to the kitchen, put a bag in the coffee-maker, filled it with water and turned it on.

"Where do you live, Dick?" I said and watched through the door how he got up from the sofa and went around the room looking at the furniture. I threw some cookies on a plate and went in without the coffee.

"In town," he said. "I live in town."

"Have a seat," I said again and offered him the cookies. "Coffee's coming up."

This time he sat down in the chair next to the sideboard. I went across and poured myself a glass of Beaujolais. Then I fetched the coffee.

"Now, then," I said. "Bob tells me you know something about Ricky Wilson and Brad Sorensen that we don't."

Dick picked up his cup and—showing more of his genteel background—slurped.

"It goes back a long time," he said. "The big oil companies—especially *Southwestern Oil*—want to increase drilling off the coast of Louisiana. The environmentalists are stubbornly opposed. They say the coastline has already been compromised by the oil companies who've dug channels into the delta, the salt water has invaded the bayous, and land is being lost at the rate of a football field every half hour. Around the clock. A hundred years from now there'll be nothing left."

His recital sounded strangely rehearsed.

"Are you from Louisiana?" I said.

"No, ma'am."

"Are you an environmentalist?"

"I'm FBI."

"Yes. Pardon me."

"About six months ago *Southwestern Oil* reported they'd received a series of anonymous threats. The threats were followed by a couple of accidents. Not workers. Engineers. The Bureau was called in to investigate."

"And Ricky Wilson?"

"Went undercover."

"Recruited after he retired?"

"Yes, ma'am."

"What did he find out?"

"Suspicious activity by a group of environmentalists who've been agitating against oil spills and contamination for the past couple of years. Seems they were ignored—if not brushed off—by the top brass. And, as I said, six months ago there were two deaths."

“And the name of the group?”

“*Citizens for Environmental Clean-Up, Now!*” Jimmy said without hesitation.

“Who were the engineers?”

“Don’t know their names. Worked on the rigs.”

“What happened to them?”

“One fell overboard and was dead when found. The other disappeared from the oil rig miles off the coast and hasn’t been found.”

“Why were these incidents treated as crimes and not as accidents?”

“I suppose the anonymous threats had something to do with it.”

“And this wasn’t picked up by the news media?”

“No, it’s been kept quiet.”

“Amazing. Thought they’d have nosed out a story like that.”

“We have our means,” Dick said.

“And Brad Sorensen was sent down pretending to be a journalist?”

“Don’t know nothin’ about that.”

Did he know about Brad’s demise or not? I left it alone.

“Anything else you can share?” I said. “Does anyone know where Ricky Wilson is?”

Dick looked uncomfortable.

“He’s gone even deeper undercover.”

“Do you know when he was last in touch?”

“Couple of days ago, ma’am.” Dick said and re-arranged his tie. The showgirl wriggled.

“Anything else you’re able to share?”

“No, ma’am. But I do have a piece of advice.”

“Which would be?”

“For your own good. Better stay away from this.”

“I’ll consider it.”

“You should,” Dick said.

“Well, Bob said you’d tell us everything you know,” I said.

"Yes, ma'am."

"And have you?"

"Can't think of anything to add," he said.

"In that case," I said and got up, "thanks for coming over."

As soon as Dickie left I stopped the tape recorder and put the tape in my desk drawer. I called Bob at the hospital.

"What did you send me?" I said.

"What do you mean?"

"He didn't look like FBI."

"They have all kinds and, believe you me, he's FBI," Bob said.

"He told me basically what we've surmised already," I said. "But said he didn't know anything about Brad Sorensen."

"Word may not have trickled down yet," Bob said.

"Maybe. What's Brad's background?"

"He and Ricky and I started at the Bureau at the same time. Brad was up in Chicago several years and then in New Orleans until three years ago."

"So he went back to the same turf. Could he have been involved with an old case?"

"Possibly," Bob said.

"Dickie said a group called *Citizens for Environmental Clean-Up, Now!* is suspected of bumping off oil company engineers around New Orleans. Started six months ago. Heard anything about that?"

"Don't think so. Didn't hit the papers I read," Bob said.

"Exactly. Wouldn't you think that's newsworthy?"

"Of course. But it could have been kept under wraps."

"Did Brad have a family?"

"Divorced as who isn't."

"Children?"

"Not that I know of."

"Are you alone?"

"No, Gwen Wilson is here. She says hello. She received your contract. I gave her our report."

"Without the gruesome details, I trust."

"Yes, without those," Bob said.

"I'm asking Martin Cook to look into the environmental group and the oil company," I said. "And how's your leg?"

"Thanks for finally asking. Looks as if I'll avoid surgery. They're trying to save me the pain."

"Why don't I call you back tomorrow when I've collected more information," I said.

"Gwen asks when you're planning to return to New Orleans? She's somewhat concerned about you down there in the hurricane season."

"Tell her I'm not worried."

Chapter 29

Downtown Washington, August 16, 2005

I blocked Susan Denzel's double punch.

I thrust both fists forward, palms facing her, and knocked her arms outward. I gripped her shoulders firmly, let out a "kihap," made sure she couldn't head-butt me, and drove my left knee into her middle. Without causing damage.

The *sensei* nodded and the line of black belt holders watched intently.

Susan and I reversed positions and I put forward my left foot and tried to punch her out with my right fist. She deflected my arm, crossed hers, made a left fist, and aimed for the side of my head. If this had been real I'd have been out cold.

Susan joined the monkey line of belts. From white to yellow, red, brown, brown/black stripe and black. I spent the next two hours doing forms, alternating between speed and force and, at the end, demonstrated my new fighting form composed for the occasion.

Sweat oozed out of all pores but I still controlled my breathing. The room was hushed as I finished the last form. I felt empowered. The ceremony was short and sweet. I tied my new black belt around my waist and the support from the room was satisfying. I'd been working five years towards this goal.

Everyone gathered around with congratulations but as soon as I'd bowed and backed out of the *dojo* I looked around for Susan Denzel to make sure she didn't leave without me.

"Are you still in Human Resources?" I said when we walked outside.

"Not any more."

"Why? What happened?"

Susan looked at me funny.

"I hear you went to New Orleans," she said.

"I had a feeling you were the one who gave Bob Makowski the information about Ricky Wilson," I said. "But he never mentioned your name."

Susan closed her eyes briefly.

"I've been reprimanded and demoted. I shouldn't have told him anything. I didn't know it was sensitive information. They should have stamped the file accordingly. Or removed it."

"I'll let Bob know. He should pull some strings."

"Oh, please. He's done enough. And to think I ever dated the guy. Should have known better."

"Not to be insensitive but as long as you've already been demoted, anything else you remember about Ricky's retirement?" I said.

"Like what?"

"Do you know him personally?"

"Some. Everyone passes through the department sooner or later."

"Did you handle his retirement?"

"I filled out the paperwork."

"Was it a sudden move?" I said.

"I had a feeling it was."

"Did he tell you why?"

"No."

"You know he's disappeared?" I said.

"No." Susan looked startled. "No, that I haven't heard."

"Will you see what you can find out?"

"Kind of hard. They have me in archives. Non-classified."

"Do you know Brad Sorensen from Special Investigations?"

"Sure. What a doll. Came in a few weeks ago to change his address."

"From where to where?"

"From Virginia to the District. He's off on a mission. He asked me out on a date but said we'd have to wait until he returned. Well, here's my car, we'll be in touch," Susan said at the next corner.

That solved the dilemma of how much to tell, and when. Bob would have to straighten this one out without me.

Downtown Washington was a sweltering humid inferno with the temperature reaching for a hundred. Leaving the air-conditioned martial arts center had been like walking into a wet blanket. It makes you wonder about the pioneers who insisted on building cities in swamps. New Orleans and Washington both. I retrieved my Jaguar from the parking garage and drove back to Bethesda.

When I got home I called Martin Cook, my personal Internet snoop. He's cute, 45, and divorced. Sometimes I feel it's too bad I don't mix business with pleasure. Until I remember he's only five-six. Anyway, now I've kind of earmarked him for Topsy.

"Hey," he said. "I've got good news and I've got bad news. Which do you want first?"

"Hard choice."

"You want your glass half full or half empty?"

"Half full if you put it that way. I'm an optimist."

Martin laughed.

"Your Doc Winnipeg a.k.a. Hubert Huffnagel heads a legitimate non-profit organization, the *Cliniques d'Haiti*, registered in Louisiana. I'm getting their financial statements shortly."

"Let me know who the donors are, will you?"

"No problem."

"And the glass you're offering which is half empty?"

"The records for the house your friend rented in New Orleans cannot be opened. I'll have to make some personal calls. See if I can smoke out the info."

"Great," I said and told Martin about *Southwestern Oil*. "I need you to get me the names of engineers working on their rigs in the Gulf."

"How soon do you need it?"

"Yesterday."

"You'll have it in the morning. Anything else?"

"Ever heard of a group called *Citizens for Environmental Clean-Up, Now!*?"

"Sorry. No."

"They're in New Orleans. I need a list of their board members and officers."

"Will do," he said. "And one more thing."

"Yes?"

"Let's have lunch next time you're downtown."

"Sure thing," I said. Maybe I could send Topsy instead.

There was plenty on Google about *Citizens for Environmental Clean-Up, Now!* Started ten years ago, their platform included insistence on the restoration of thousands of canals dug by oil companies in the Louisiana delta. I found records of numerous federal lawsuits concerning air and water pollution. Scads of letters to senators and government officials with some unfortunate phrases which made the environmentalists sound like crackpots. I spent another hour scouring newspaper articles but found nothing about dead engineers.

Next I googled *Southwestern Oil*. Their website informed me of their products and services, how concerned they were about the environment, the names and photos of the four top honchos—looking remarkably alike—but nothing else I could use. I'd wait for Martin Cook's report.

My call to the lab down on L Street did nothing to relieve my frustration. The tests on the vial found in Ricky's living room were inconclusive. Not enough residue, apparently, but for me to check back in six days.

My last call went to Bob.

"Brad Sorensen was going to date Susan Denzel when he returned from New Orleans." I said. "And she's been reprimanded and removed from temptation in Human Resources to non-classified archives."

"Geez," Bob said.

"You need to be more contrite."

"I'll take her out to lunch."

"Brilliant," I said.

"I'll talk to someone," he said.

"Don't. You've done enough already," I said.

"I'll still do something," Bob said.

"Okay, I believe you," I said. "But that's not really why I'm calling. I need someone in New Orleans with clout."

"Or someone in Washington with clout in New Orleans?"

"Exactly."

"Patricia Underwood," Bob said.

"It's time for you to call in her debt."

And I explained to Bob what I needed from the Congresswoman from Louisiana. As soon as we hung up I reserved a flight to New Orleans for the next afternoon.

Chapter 30

New Orleans, August 17, 2005

"He'll see you now, Ms. Harcourt," the receptionist said.

That's what my fake press pass said. Ruth Harcourt. The name didn't fit my personality. I pictured Ruth as short, dark, intense, in a black tailored suit and sensible shoes while I'm tall, blonde, and slim, and possessed of a black belt. But that's what Martin Cook had been able to come up with on short notice. I was affiliated with the *Washington Post*, free-lance. My business card looked impressive, courtesy of Martin. The phone number went straight to his office.

The *Southwestern Oil* company executive offices were hidden away in a park with scraggly trees to the south of New Orleans. With my unfailing talent for getting lost on highways and subsidiary roads it had taken me two hours to get there. From afar the building looked like a prison minus the watch tower. The walls were gray, the roof was flat and the windows recessed. Not a place I'd enjoy being trapped during working hours. Or after.

The inside of the building wasn't much more inviting. The elevators were hidden around far corners and the reception area looked grim. I was the only visitor.

Frank Smith, Public Relations, greeted me on the third floor with a bland handshake. He was fifty-ish with pale comb-over hair, small eyes and an unfortunate nose. He showed me into his office and pointed me to a leather chair. He sat down opposite me. He studied my card and placed it on the glass coffee table.

"You're writing a series of articles about oil rigs," he said. Talked through his teeth. Looked verklemt.

"That's right." I gave him my roving reporter smile. Toothy and white.

"Patricia Underwood was a little vague about who *The Post* would be sending and the exact nature of your article but she's a good friend of mine."

"She'll be appreciative of the fact that you've received me so promptly," I said.

"Her wish is my command."

"She represents the people of your fair state admirably," I said.

"She's a fine woman," he said.

And blah, blah, blah.

I crossed my legs and Frank Smith took a good look up my skirt. Dressed to kill.

"You're my last stop," I said. "I've boned up on platform types—fixed, semi-submersibles, jack-ups, tension-legs, and seastars—and on maintenance and risks."

"You've got the vocabulary right."

"The history of oil exploration is fascinating," I said. "I've read about the Oil Rocks on the Caspian Sea which is a city of five thousand people. Hard to imagine. I also know that the first modern offshore rigs were drilling in the Gulf by 1947. And I'm fascinated by the story of "Mr. Charlie" from the 1950s."

"Ah," Frank Smith said. "Revolutionized the offshore oil industry in the Gulf. The first of the semisubmersibles."

"Sceptics didn't think it was possible. To have a barge over two hundred feet long wholly self-sufficient," I said repeating some of my readings.

"You did your homework," Frank Smith said.

If he only knew how recently and how superficially.

"And now I'm ready to visit an actual rig," I said.

"All right," Frank Smith said. "No doubt Patricia told you that we're not really interested in publicity. We like to keep a low profile."

"Understood," I said.

"You'll have no problem running the article by me before it's printed?"

"No problem at all."

Especially since no article would be written.

"Excellent."

"Although I imagine that accidents are unavoidable both to personnel and machinery on an oil rig. The public is aware of that," I said.

"I can assure you we're transparent on those issues—labor unions, OSHA, insurance companies see to that—but I quite understand if you need to touch on that subject. In a general way, of course, briefly."

"Of course. But listen," I said, "I hope my article isn't going to end up as *deja vu* all over again. Has any other journalist talked to you in the last month or so about this subject?"

Frank Smith got up and moved to his recessed window. He looked out for quite a while. The architecture was designed to let in no light whatsoever but maybe he was interested in the flock of birds I'd seen circle the building. Probably vultures.

"Not that I know of," he said and returned to his chair.

"Could it have escaped your attention?"

"No, what I meant to say was that no other journalist has shown any interest."

"That's a relief," I said. "I hate to be up-ended. There's this Ricky Wilson from *The New York Times*. You haven't come across him, have you?"

"Who?"

"Ricky Wilson."

I watched his face carefully. Not a flicker. He was either very good or he'd never heard the name.

"Never heard of him," Frank Smith said.

I was fairly certain that Brad Sorensen had used a fake name. One I didn't know. But I had to try it anyway.

"Then there's Brad Sorensen also from the *Times*. Come across him?"

"Never heard of him either," Frank Smith said. He picked up my business card from the coffee table.

"*The Washington Post* has my utmost respect," he said. "But the paper is known for its probing investigations."

I crossed my legs the other way and he took another peek. I have no shame in the line of duty. Might prevent him from bringing up Watergate and Woodward and Bernstein.

"I'm on a very tight schedule," I said. "Came here on the spur of the moment. Was supposed to visit Prince Edward Island but the story of the Irving Whale disaster has been widely covered and, anyway, happened a long time ago."

"And the Exxon Valdez," Frank Smith said. "We've had nothing like that happen here."

"Exactly," I said. "My articles will address the human interest angle. My focus will be on the people who work on the rigs, their backgrounds, their families, their attitudes. From a sociological standpoint, you understand."

Frank Smith suddenly was inspired to leave his chair.

"How about right now," he said and reached for the phone.

"You have time right now?"

"Yes. We'll pay a visit to the nearest floating rig. Did you bring a photographer?"

"I'm my own chronicler," I said. "Both in writing and in the picturesque. I brought my camera. And I'm ready to go."

Chapter 31

"That's the pipe deck." Frank Smith pointed down from where we stood on the upper rig floor.

The helicopter had dropped us at the rig's heliport just above the crew quarters. The machinery and equipment on the deck looked mysterious.

"Mud tanks, mud pumping units and bulk tanks," Frank Smith said and adjusted his hardhat.

The entire rig resembled the skeleton of an unfinished Erector Set. Cable and hoisting mechanisms ran up the huge cranes. The buoyancy tanks below the surface of the water strained against the cable anchors. A stiff wind blew right through the rig. I could sense the platform float, my feet felt as if they couldn't get a good grip on the deck.

"It's perfectly stable," Frank Smith said. He was white in the face. I felt a bit queasy myself. "The anchors weigh upwards of ten tons."

"The rig is movable?"

"Sure, that's the beauty of the semisubmersible rig."

"How does it work?" I took out my notebook and poised my pen.

"I'll give you some literature. In a nutshell, the buoyancy tanks can be deflated or inflated but the rig still floats. It can be moved from place to place. During drilling the tanks keep the rig stable."

"What happens in stormy weather? You're in the middle of hurricane season now. What precautions are you taking?"

"We fasten the bolts and cross our fingers." Frank Smith looked around for a place to sit.

"The crew quarters are on the two decks below. There's a cafeteria, a gym, a TV gameroom, bathrooms, showers, and sleeping quarters. Offices."

"The crews sleep here?"

"They work in seven day shifts, twelve hour day or night shifts. Then they're off seven days."

I wrote in my notebook.

"And the best people for me to interview would be?"

"Interview?"

"I'd like to speak directly to a couple. Human interest stories."

"An engineer, then."

"Good."

"I'll round up a subsea engineer or a mud engineer."

"How about one of those?" I pointed to a brawny guy in a yellow hardhat holding a blowtorch.

"The welder?"

"Yes."

"Shouldn't be a problem. Let's find out when he's on a break."

Half an hour later I sat in the cafeteria with a cup of very black coffee opposite Ben Williams, the rig's chief engineer. Frank Smith was peering into his cup with a frown. Looked like his stomach was telling him no. Everywhere on the rig one could feel the heaving movements under the floor. Frank Smith excused himself after making his introductions and I again poised my pen above my notebook.

"How long have you been with the oil company, Mr. Williams," I began.

"Just call me Ben."

"Thank you."

"Been with the company fifteen years this coming November."

"You live in New Orleans?"

"Sure. The wife's a librarian. We've got two kids in high school."

"I understand you work seven days and take off seven?"

"That's right. I finish my tour this evening. Helicopter leaves at six."

I made a mental note.

"What's your background, Ben?"

"Engineering degree from Louisiana State in Baton Rouge. Experience in pneumatics and hydraulics."

"And your duties on the rig?"

"I'm in charge of the motion compensation system of the rig, the marine riser and the blow out preventer. I deal with equipment repair and emergency procedures."

"So, you're responsible for safety onboard?"

"Yes. Prevention of damage to the rig and to loss of life."

I saw Frank Smith weave across the floor. But instead of joining us he sat at a far table and smoothed back his dwindling hair. Looked washed out.

"And how's the record?"

Ben Williams looked across the cafeteria at Frank Smith who got up from his table and disappeared towards the bathrooms.

"I'm sure Mr. Smith told you that he'll see my article before it's printed," I said.

"He did. But there's no need for secrecy. We haven't had any loss to property or crew since 2001."

"What happened then?"

"We had a fire which was contained after three hours," Ben Williams said.

"But no 'man overboard' or anything like that?"

"That's right."

"How about on the other rigs? Any close calls there?"

Ben Williams looked around the cafeteria but didn't find the reassuring figure of Frank Smith.

"Can't really speak to that," he said.

"Fair enough," I said and reluctantly changed the topic. "Tell me, how do you prepare for the hurricane season?"

"Tie down the bolts and cross our fingers."

Seemed to be the official line.

"Is that sufficient?" I said.

"There's a lot of hype this time of year. Every year. The winds change from hour to hour. The forecasters all admit hurricane prediction is an inexact science."

"I'm with you," I said. "Hoping for the best, I mean."

Frank Smith returned with the hefty welder in tow and Ben, the engineer, got up.

"Pleasure to meet you. Take care," he said and the welder took his place.

This time Frank Smith sat down as well.

"Abbott, this is Ms. Harcourt," he said to the welder. "A journalist from *The Washington Post*."

I'd nearly forgotten my *nom de plume*. In most cases using a false name is not a good idea. There's always the chance that your first-grade teacher or your next-door neighbor will spot you and out you. Maybe not a big chance of that on an oil rig, though.

"How long have you been a welder, Abbott?"

"Some twenty years, Miss."

"And how long on this rig?"

"Five years."

"And what are your duties exactly?"

"I repair the metalwork. I weld pipes."

"Dangerous work?"

"You got to pay attention. There's high pressure in the pipes."

"Accidents will happen anyway, I imagine?"

Abbott looked briefly at Frank Smith.

"It's okay," Frank said.

"Sometimes," Abbott said. "But nothing fatal."

"You don't have people falling overboard, I imagine?" I laughed to indicate the joking nature of my question.

"No, nothing like that." Abbott got my joke and laughed.

"What about other rigs?"

"I wouldn't know about that, Miss." Abbott was starting to look uncomfortable.

"You work twelve hour shifts for seven days. How does your family handle your schedule?" I said.

"Glad to be rid of me for a week at a time."

"You married with children?"

"Married. No children."

Abbott returned to his welding and Frank Smith and I toured the rest of the crew quarters. I made copious notes and took scads of digital photos. I got Ben Williams and Abbott to pose in front of various machinery.

"I meant to ask you about your trouble with the environmentalists," I said to Frank Smith as we went back up to the heliport on the upper rig floor.

"What do you mean? What trouble?"

"Something I read in the *Picayune-Times* a while back."

"You must be referring to the nuts at *Citizens for Environmental Clean-Up, Now!*"

"Yes, that sounds like the name."

The helicopter blades whirred and stirred up a gale. Frank Smith preceded me up the steps. When we were strapped in he turned to me.

"Take it from me. If you've read or heard his rantings you'd dismiss him off-hand."

"Who?"

"Pete Brogan. Their so-called leader."

"Pete Brogan?" I repeated. "Does he by any chance run a tourist ferry boat service in the bayou?"

"Ah, you know him?"

"Know of him but didn't know about him being an environmentalist."

"He's a marine biologist. Used to teach at Tulane University. He got fired. Now he's a ferry boat operator and an environmentalist. Assisted by his crackpot wife."

Chapter 32

After leaving Frank Smith at the executive offices of *Southewestern Oil* I went back to the helicopter landing pad near the docks. Waiting for six o'clock and Ben Williams, the engineer.

While I waited I checked my cell phone messages.

"*Citizens for Environmental Clean-Up, Now!* is run by a guy by the name of Peter Brogan," Martin Cook said.

Old news.

"Their website says they're having a big rally in New Orleans at nine this evening. Write down this address."

Good news.

I checked the address on my city map. Up towards the Superdome. Shouldn't be hard to find. While I folded and re-folded the map into the wrong pleats I noticed a gray Chevy roll up and park to the left of me. A large dark shape slumped in the driver's seat.

There was a message from Bob Makowski and one from Topsy. The last message was another from Martin Cook.

"Write down these names," Martin said and gave me the names of sixteen engineers on eight different rigs belonging to *Southwestern Oil*. "I checked the obituaries for the last six months," he continued. "One deceased. Engineer by the name of Rowland Brown. Fifty-three years old. The obit said suddenly departed."

At six-twenty the helicopter landed and disgorged about fifteen men. I left my car and walked to the gate. Ben Williams was the third one through.

"Mr. Williams," I said. "Ben."

He stopped short and didn't look glad to see me. He started up again and walked towards a green Honda.

"Ben," I said and walked as fast as he. "Can you give me another few minutes?"

"Not really," he said and opened the door to his car. "Wouldn't be appropriate without Frank Smith."

I opened the door to his passenger seat and jumped in. Ben looked at me in despair.

"I realize journalists have to be aggressive," he said. "But I really have nothing else to tell you."

He was much too nice to force me out of his car and I almost felt sorry for him. But not too sorry. I had a job to do as an aggressive journalist.

I pulled out Ricky Wilson's photograph. Which could just as well have been Brad Sorensen's.

"Please take a good look. Ever seen this guy before?"

Ben Williams took a good look and shook his head.

"Can't say that I have. What's going on. You some kind of investigator?"

"No," I lied. "This guy is the competition. Journalist with *The New York Times.* I'm trying to make sure he isn't writing the same article. I'm free lance and write on speculation. Investing my own time and money."

"I see," Ben said.

"You're absolutely sure?"

"I'm absolutely sure. And I really want to get going."

"I'll let you go in a moment," I said. "Rowland Brown a friend of yours?"

Ben Williams looked truly startled.

"Yes. How do you know about him?" he said.

"It was in the paper. Where did it happen?"

"Onboard the new rig. Not mine."

"Was it a suspicious accident?"

"No. It wasn't an accident."

"What happened?" I said.

"He had a heart attack."

"You mean he had a heart attack and fell overboard?"

Ben Williams looked at me and shook his head.

"Where do you people get your misinformation?" he said and started up his car. "Rowland Brown had a heart attack. He did not fall overboard. He was in the cafeteria when it happened."

He revved up the car.

"I'd like to get started for home now if you don't mind," he said.

"Thanks, Ben," I said. "Just one more thing. Did Rowland Brown live in New Orleans?"

"He was from Baton Rouge. Please close the door."

Ben Williams took off in an indignant cloud of dust and I returned to my car.

The drive back to New Orleans took forty minutes. I contemplated the back of a nineteen-twenties gangster car with fake bullet holes while a car built like a WWI ambulance passed me on the left. The automotive industry has come a long way, baby.

The gray Chevy from the helicopter parking lot was right behind me. I know a tail when I see one and this one was an amateur. Should've stayed at least two cars behind me. But the faux ambulance had pulled out to pass me and left the Chevy in full view. In my rearview mirror the driver was still slumped over the wheel and wore dark sunglasses.

The road opened up in front of me but I didn't speed up. In fact, I slowed down to about 45 mph. There was some tooting going on behind me and a line of cars passed me but not the Chevy. Go on, man, the rules of tailing say just pass me and I won't suspect you. But, no, he stayed right behind me.

I swung into the next *Southwestern Oil* gas station at the last moment. Not at the entrance but at the exit, against traffic.

The Chevy driver applied his brakes but had to pass. I filled the car and got back on the road. The Chevy was waiting in the breakdown lane half a mile away. He pulled in three cars behind me. An amateur I couldn't seem to shake.

I parked the car in the Monteleone garage, shed my Ms. Ruth Harcourt image and emerged in the lobby as Ms. Jamie Prescott.

I ordered room service, ate and showered and prepared my evening personality.

At a quarter to eight—in a brown wig, jogging suit and glasses—I got in a taxi and went to the *Citizens for Environmental Clean-Up, Now!* rally.

My tail in the gray Chevy paid me no attention.

Chapter 33

It was dark as the taxi went straight across Canal Street to St. Charles Avenue, took a right on Poydras, crossed Loyola, and went to the address a block from City Hall. The street was crowded with people entering the meeting hall. A green and white banner flapped hard against the wall above the entrance saying "Action, Now!" A muscular arm—as seen in Workers Unite posters of yore—ended in a clenched fist.

Being tall has its advantages but not when you're trying to blend into a crowd of people decidedly at the lower end of average. My flat heels didn't feel flat enough. There was only so much I could do by slouching. That's why I sat down in the back row as soon as I was inside the meeting hall. Tugged at my wig which felt as if it was crawling with ants. The air-conditioning was most likely on somewhere but didn't reach the back row.

Seemed that everyone knew one another. There was a good deal of shouting and back-slapping before people settled down. The meeting had been announced for nine o'clock but by nine-thirty nothing had happened on the stage. The speaker's podium was still empty. Someone ran across to test the microphone and it didn't work. Someone else ran across and re-arranged the wires. At nine forty-five a woman stepped up on the podium.

"We're here tonight to address some serious issues and to report to you on some recent results," she began.

There was a small commotion at the entrance and I missed the next few sentences. A couple of people were shown out. Must be the opposition preparing to interrupt.

". . . and a hearty welcome to our president, Peter Brogan," the woman concluded. She stepped back and applauded as Cap'n Pete took up his position on the podium.

Loud applause from the hall. And some boos. Lively evening coming up. Every seat was taken. Standing room only at the back of the hall which happened to be a few feet away from my row. Several tough guys in black with batons now guarded the entrance. A murmur ran through the hall.

Peter Brogan, the environmentalist, looked quite different from the captain of the ferry boat. His speech was no longer colloquial, here was an educated man holding forth about his convictions. He changed into an orator in front of my eyes. Voice rising and falling, suggestive pauses. He grabbed the mike and paced across the stage pointing at the audience. Railing against wetland destruction, oil spills, flood control, spillways, chemical plants, air pollution, global warming.

There was much more and after a while my eyes glazed over—no doubt because I wasn't sufficiently familiar with the nitty-gritty of the subject matter—but the audience went wild and interrupted with shouts of encouragement.

The trouble started in the middle of the hall. People were standing, there was punching and shouting and Pete Brogan's voice rose to be heard. He swung a gavel on the podium to no effect. The meeting was breaking up. He banged the gavel until the woman who'd introduced him ran across the stage and grabbed his arm. She dragged him away.

I stood up thinking I'd better leave. I turned around and came face to face with Monique Jones, the voudou queen of *Blue Grotto* fame. Just behind her was Doc Winnipeg. I hadn't seen them as environmentalists. Go figure. She looked exotic in a red bandana, matching nailpolish, and a long dress in a silky blue material. The Doc's gray hair flowed unhindered around his pale face. He looked right past me.

I sat down abruptly and squinted at the floor. A brown wig does wonders. Or maybe it was the glasses. They do make me look mousy. When I turned my head to see if I'd been outed all I saw was their backs. They struggled through the crowd towards a stage door. I got up again and fought my way to the exit.

The hall was now in full uproar. Bottles were crashing. People were screaming. A lot were scrambling to get out my exit door but I got there first.

Outside I re-adjusted my wig and went up the street as the sirens signaled the arrival of the police coming to quell the uprising. I climbed the stoop of a one-story building from where I got a good view of the police entering the meeting hall and people trying to escape. Several shots were fired inside the building. Three ambulances pulled through the crowd prepared for victims.

Then nothing happened. After a short while the cops came back out and drove away. The three ambulances left for lack of injured. A tight group of basketball players—at least I assumed they were basketball players seeing they all looked eight feet tall—meandered down the front steps. Three serious-looking students carried banners in obvious defeat. Half a dozen men with hanging bellies shouted slogans and disappeared down the street with an aura of mission accomplished. Five women in hippie-dresses conferred half-heartedly before disbursing. The town was slowly back to normal and the meeting had been successfully broken up.

I went up another two steps on the stoop and settled in. I could see an exit on the side of the building and unless Pete Brogan left by a back door I would spot him. I removed my brown wig and stuffed it in my pocket together with the granny glasses, shook out my hair and gave it a quick comb-through with my fingers.

Half an hour later Pete Brogan, Yvette, his wife—looking square and severe—Monique and Doc Winnipeg came out the door together and joined the thinning crowd on the other side of the street.

I walked across and stopped in front of them.

Chapter 34

"Hi, everyone," I said.

"Uh," Monique said.

"Jamie Prescott," I said to help her out. "Hi Pete, Mrs. Brogan, Doc Winnipeg. Fancy meeting you all here."

They stared and I smiled.

Pete Brogan found his voice first. The one he used on the ferry boat.

"What a surprise. Thought you'd gone back up north with your friend the FBI man."

"Former," I said. "Former FBI man."

"Yes. How is his leg?" Pete said.

"Thanks for asking. He's back in Washington recovering in the hospital."

"What's wrong with him?" Doc Winnipeg said.

"Broke his leg falling off Pete's ferry boat," I said.

The doc looked at Pete Brogan.

"You didn't mention that," he said.

"No need," Pete said. "He fell. It was an accident. He didn't want me to make a big deal of it."

I looked from Pete to Doc Winnipeg and back to Pete. There was some kind of relationship here that I couldn't figure out. But I would as soon as I could put my mind to it. Monique and Pete's wife didn't seem to have anything in common. They didn't even look at one another.

We started walking.

"Has anyone heard from Ricky Wilson?" I asked.

"Not me." Monique sounded definite.

"Me either," Doc Winnipeg said.

"I thought you found him," Pete Brogan's wife said.

"No, Mother. That was someone else," Pete said to her.

"What do you mean," Doc said.

Pete stared him down.

"Who was the someone else?" Doc repeated.

"None of your business," Pete Brogan said and steered his wife towards a car parked at the curb. He got her into the passenger seat and waved his hand in a definite goodbye.

"Enjoy the meeting?" I said to Monique.

"Sucked," she said. "I'm not getting dragged back there again. Bunch of nuts."

"How did the fight start?" I said.

"How do you know about the fight," Doc Winnipeg said.

"Happened to be at the meeting," I said.

"Then you saw what went on." He stared at me with his dead fish eyes. "Why were you there?"

"Why were *you*?" I said. "Are you an environmentalist?"

"It's one of my interests," he said. "And you?"

"Sounded like an interesting public event," I said. "I hear that *Citizens for Environmental Clean-Up, Now!* is having some trouble with *Southwestern Oil*. Do you know anything about that?"

"Bloodsuckers," Doc said.

"So, who started the fight?" I said again.

"Who knows. A bunch of thugs."

"Come on," Monique said and started walking. Doc Winnipeg smiled at me with his disgusting teeth and followed her. They made an interesting pair from the back. She—in her flowing skirt which clung to her thighs—looked like a ragdoll. He—in a black suit, white tie, and a Panama hat—was scarecrow incarnate. They turned at the first corner and were gone.

The door to the meeting hall opened again and a small group of men was briefly illuminated by the lights inside. The last one slammed the door shut and they ambled down the steps laughing and jostling. I stood still at the curb and watched them. Five burly guys in motor cycle leather and one thin man wearing black jeans and a tight black shirt. The other five kept a respectful distance around him and I knew immediately who he was. The chicken killer, Toussaint.

I hauled the brown wig out of my pocket, clamped it on my head, and put on my granny glasses. Then I let the group get far enough down the street before I followed. They walked boisterously towards Canal Street and turned down Bourbon Street. I slouched behind them about a hundred feet or so not really trusting my disguise. I reflected silently on genes and on my mother and her tall Swedish ancestors. Usually a good thing but not so good tonight. My father—who'd been short Italian and French—would have been more helpful.

The closer we got to the *Blues Grotto* the more I understood what was going on. And when the toughs and Toussaint went down the alley to the side entrance I wasn't exactly surprised. Under the leather they were blues musicians. When I last met them two of them were gorillas.

I was about to follow them inside when Jon Douglas, carrying his sax, walked to the same side entrance with Monique and Doc Winnipeg, The show was about to begin and all my new friends seemed to be attending. Except for the priestess, Antoinette.

I gave the show a miss and walked slowly back to the Monteleone. My tail in the gray Chevy was gone. The night was still young but I'd had it. I went upstairs to soak in the tub hoping steam would enhance my thought processes. It didn't.

The phone rang just before midnight.

"You're back in town," Jon Douglas said.

"Word travels fast," I said.

"We've got a few friends in common."

"I had a feeling," I said.
"Ready to go dancing?"
"Sure," I said. "How about tomorrow?"
"I'll pick you up at ten," he said. "Good night."

Chapter 35

New Orleans, August 18, 2005

"We've been had," Bob said.

"We've been had?"

"Screwed over."

"What do you mean?"

It was seven in the morning but I was painfully wide awake.

"What do you mean?" I repeated.

"Had a visitor at the hospital."

"This early?

"My former supervisor with some confidential news. Seems Dick was part of a set-up."

"Hot damn."

"Never was a connection to the oil companies or to the environmentalists. Total fabrication."

"Damn."

"Came all this way to tell me 'cause he didn't want me to look like a fool, he said. And I'm extending that privilege to you."

"I'm touched," I said. "And furious. I knew there was something phony about that little weasel."

"You were right. Nothing like feminine intuition."

"Excuse me? It's called professional acumen," I said. "What else did your former supervisor tell you?"

"Wouldn't give me the low-down on Ricky."

"A real friend."

"Not exactly. He's actually a nasty bastard. He must have an angle. Just can't figure out what it is."

"Could it be we're getting too close to something to do with the oil company?"

"Could be. They didn't figure on you going back to New Orleans."

"Sounds like something the Congresswoman is involved in," I said.

"Won't even help to take her out to lunch," Bob said. "She doesn't owe me anymore."

"You might still be able to exercise your charm."

"Which is considerable."

"That it is," I said.

"Although diminished by a broken leg."

"She might feel sorry for you and spill the beans."

"Not her. You don't get to Congress being nice. She's a barracuda."

"So it was all a waste of time," I said.

"Not entirely. Look at it this way. You got to visit an oil rig. Not everyone's so lucky."

"Sure. Mudlocks. Mudtanks. Motion compressor systems. Blow-out preventers."

"What?"

"Semi-submersibles. Jack-ups. Tension-legs. Knowledge I can't live without."

"Nothing wrong with a general education I always say."

"Never heard you say that. I'll send you some photos. Took about a hundred."

"Don't bother," Bob said.

"Seems we've hit an important nerve," I said.

"That's for sure. I was told once more to stop interfering."

"And will you?"

"You want to throw in the towel?"

"No way, José."

Bob laughed.

"Back to square one then?"

"Absolutely. Look, let me reorganize my thoughts and call you back."

"I'm lying here in traction waiting impatiently," Bob said. "Oh, and one more thing. Gwen Wilson sends her regards. Says she's still worrying about the hurricane threat."

"Tell her not to worry. I'm fastening the bolts."

"What?"

"Yes, and crossing my fingers."

Since sleep was now impossible I ordered room service. Orange-juice, croissants, and coffee. I waited twenty minutes before the waiter stood in front of the only free tabletop in the room. A loaded tray was perched on his right shoulder.

"Where d'you want it," he said.

"On the floor."

"Oh, joke," he said but didn't laugh. Probably too early in the day. I added a tip and signed the bill.

I ate a leathery croissant and downed the coffee while I re-organized my thoughts. Not that easy. I had been so intent on Frank Smith's evasions, Ben Williams and Abbott's apparent fear of telling me too much. Rowland Brown's death was probably caused by a bona fide heart attack. But if everything was on the up and up why did Frank Smith put a tail on me? Had he called *The Post* to verify my existence? If so, it wouldn't be long before Congresswoman Patricia Underwood demanded an explanation from Bob.

And who knew what other sinister secrets Frank Smith had. The oil companies were at war with the environmentalists. Everyone knew that. The break-up of the rally last night had definitely been engineered. By whom? No longer my problem. Time to switch focus.

Chapter 36

The early morning news concentrated the entire weather report on a storm about to transform itself into a hurricane moving around in the Gulf. They were talking about hurricane Betsy in 1965 which had flooded New Orleans. Quoting officials telling folks to hang tight, fasten the bolts, cross their fingers.

At eight Bob called me back.

"I've had a complaint about you," he said. "Patricia Underwood wants to know why I sent a fake journalist to dupe her good friend Frank Smith into revealing state secrets. Know anything about that?"

"No. Must've been a friend of mine. You remember Ruth Harcourt, roving reporter."

"No, I don't. She happen to rove on an oil rig in the Gulf?"

"Yeah, she roved and roved and got nowhere."

"I'll tell the Congresswoman. She wants me to get back to her."

"I told you. She may want to pump you or scold you or both, but you could still take her out to lunch. It's one of your best moves."

"I'll totally disown you."

"Feel free," I said.

"Where do we go from here?" Bob said.

"Why don't you recapitulate?" I said. "Just to clear my sinuses and make sure I haven't missed anything."

"Fine. Ricky Wilson retires to New Orleans. He's recruited back by the Bureau. Goes undercover but is unable to change his identity since he's already known to a lot of people. He's played with two jazz bands that we know of. At Monique's *Blues Grotto* and at *Jake's*. He's reported to be feeding the drums and putting them to bed at Priestess Antoinette's voudou establishment. He disappears."

"He uses an, as yet, unidentified drug," I said.

"Does it matter?"

"Maybe not."

"Brad Sorensen is sent down by the Bureau with a fake name that we haven't discovered yet. He may have posed as a reporter. He's found his way to Antoinette's and even gets the honor of playing one of the drums. Not very expertly. He get's into a car with Louisiana plates and drives across the Mississippi River towards swamp country."

"Did you trace the plates?" I said.

"No need. They don't exist. Part of his fake identity."

"Same is true for the owners of Ricky's house. FBI."

"We follow Brad Sorensen. He escapes in a motorboat. Someone—or several people—follow him. He's killed and left in the bayou. The killers sink Brad's boat and return to the dock. They drive his car away. Probably remove the plates and abandon it."

"And," I said, "we don't know if the killers have caught up with Ricky Wilson."

"If I know Ricky he's lying low somewhere."

"Your dirty rat, Dickie, said the FBI had heard from Ricky a few days ago. We can't trust that information any more."

"I'll ask around. Carefully." Bob said.

"And we have the questions Martin Cook is looking into. Doc Winnipeg's organization. What really happened to Rowland Brown. Who's Brandy Gregory and where is she. Things like that."

"Enough stuff to keep you busy."

"I'm calling the Hibernia National Bank to double-check on Brandy Gregory," I said.

"Yeah, the one with the fake address."

"Maybe you got the street number wrong?" I said.

"Wouldn't be the first time."

"I'll call you back later," I said.

There was no one with the name Brandy Gregory in the New Orleans phone book. And the phone company didn't have a listing. A few minutes after nine I called the Hibernia National Bank and talked to the operator.

"I'm very upset," I said.

"Yes, ma'am?"

"I've given you my new address and you still can't get it right. I'm not receiving my statements in the mail."

"One moment, please. I'll connect you to the right person."

The right person came on the line after about thirty seconds of elevator music.

"How can I help you?" the woman said.

"My name is Brandy Gregory," I said. "Over two months ago I gave you my address at 3200 Baronne Alley and I have yet to receive my statements in the mail."

"One moment, please. What is the account number?"

I gave it to her.

"One moment, please."

I got the benefit of some more elevator music.

"And is this account in your name, Miss Gregory?"

"It certainly is. And in the name of Ricky Wilson."

"I'm sorry but I can't give you any information on the phone. You'd have to come to the bank with your ID."

"This is a little awkward for me. You see, I've broken my leg and can't get around."

"Sorry to hear that but we do have our rules."

"And your name is?" I said.

"My name is Denise."

"Thank you, Denise. I'll have someone drive me down to the bank."

She hung up.

I called the bank again.

"The mail room, please," I said.

"You mean the Statement Dispatch Room?"

"Yes, that's the one."

More elevator music.

"Dispatch," a woman said.

"Hello. I have a question. Denise upstairs told me to call you. My name is Brandy Gregory and this is my account number." I gave her the number.

"One moment, please. Yes, I've got you here. What's your question?"

"My question is this. It's getting rather upsetting. You see, I'm not receiving my statements at my address at 3200 Baronne Alley. I just wanted you to confirm that you have the correct address."

"Did you say 3200 Baronne Alley?"

"Yes."

"In Baton Rouge?"

In Baton Rouge?

"Yes," I said and sat down hard on my chair.

"That's where we're sending your statements," she said.

"It must be the fault of the post office then. I'll complain to them. Thanks so much for your help."

"No problem," my gullible woman said and hung up.

Baton Rouge. Brandy Gregory did not live in New Orleans. What a little deception will do for you. Skip-tracing can be a satisfying occupation. Baronne Alley showed up on the map off of Main Street near St. Joseph's Cathedral in downtown Baton Rouge.

I followed up this success by finding Rowland Brown's address on Laurel Street which ran parallel to Main. Very convenient. It would keep me from getting lost in the suburbs.

Might as well kill those two birds with one well-aimed stone.

I left the hotel at nine-thirty and headed to Baton Rouge. French for "Red Stick."

Chapter 37

Baton Rouge, August 19, 2005

The Red Stick Café in downtown Baton Rouge served brunch until eleven. Eggs Sardou turned out to be two poached eggs on artichoke bottoms with spinach and hollandaise sauce. I had it with rolls and butter and coffee topped up three times. A good brunch never hurt anyone.

The drive from New Orleans had taken an hour and a half on Interstate 10 which took me straight to downtown. The river sent in a warm breeze and I could hear the tugging of boats. The oil people were as busy here as they were in New Orleans. If not more.

It was a short walk from the café to Rowland Brown's address on Laurel Street. The houses sat close together with small yards in front and everyone apparently working since I saw no one lolling on the stoops. There was an air of history and some gentle restoration. All in all where I'd expect an educated engineer to live.

Mrs. Brown, the widow, opened the door wide without a thought to crime. In her fifties, graying hair, slim, not bad looking.

"Oh," she said and closed the door so that I couldn't look inside the hallway. "I was expecting my sister. Can I help you?"

"Sorry to intrude," I said and took out my Ruth Harcourt business card. "Frank Smith from *Southwestern Oil* gave me your address."

"Frank Smith did?"

"Yes. I'm writing a series of articles about the oil rigs and since your late husband was one of the old-timers Frank thought you might have some early photographs of him on the first rigs."

"That's unbelievable," Mrs. Brown said. "Frank Smith sent me a reporter?"

"Do you mind if I come in for a moment?"

"I certainly do. I have absolutely nothing to say to you and you can tell Frank Smith to go to hell."

She slammed the door.

Thought I'd wait for the sister to arrive so I went a few houses down the street to do that. Hard to hide without a car on a street with no pedestrians. I went past a few more houses but not so far that I couldn't intercept the sister when her car pulled up.

A woman came walking briskly up the street, her heels clicking confidently. She gave me a friendly nod when she passed me and I took a chance.

"You Rowland Brown's sister-in-law?" I said and went to her side.

She stopped and eyed me carefully.

"Who wants to know?" she said.

I pulled out my Ruth Harcourt identity.

"Frank Smith from *Southwestern Oil* told me to look up Mrs. Brown," I said. "But she told me to wait for you."

"Why would she do that? What's going on?"

"Walk with me back to the corner," I said, "and I'll tell you."

She went with me.

"I don't like Frank Smith," I said. "Something fishy going on and I believe Rowland Brown was a victim of foul play."

"You don't know my name," Rowland's sister-in-law said. "And you won't quote me?"

"Absolutely not," I said. "Your identity is safe with me."

"Rowland didn't have a heart attack," she whispered as if Frank Smith could hear her.

"It was an accident?"

"Yes. He was about to get fired. After twenty-two years on the job. Fired."

"Why?"

"He got involved with environmental issues. Talked out loud about oil spills, the swamp lands, marine life."

"And you can't do that when you work for the oil company?"

"Apparently not. It's not a free country down here," she said and sniffled.

"How do you know it was an accident?" I said.

"His head was in bandages. They said he fell after he had his heart attack."

"But you don't believe them?"

"We have a witness."

"Did anyone contact you afterwards?" I said.

"What, like reporters?"

"Yes. Someone called Ricky Wilson."

I pulled out Ricky's photograph which could stand in for Brad Sorensen.

She shook her head.

"Never seen him before."

"And what is Frank Smith's role in this?"

"Said the company would compensate my sister. Pay her a life annuity in addition to Rowland's pension. She hasn't seen a dime yet."

"Here," I said and wrote my cell phone number on the back of Ruth Harcourt's card. That's the trouble with deceitful behavior. It turns around and bites you in the ass. I'd have to remember who I was supposed to be if and when she called.

"Let me know if your sister gets the compensation she deserves," I said.

"Just don't tell anyone I talked to you," she said and stuck my card in her pocket.

Then she walked quickly to her sister's house.

Chapter 38

"A tropical storm is moving into higher latitudes from the Atlantic towards the Gulf of Mexico. It is hoped it will recurve to the north and northeast which should occur if it encounters a low-pressure system moving from west to east. That is, if the storm does not encounter currents of warmer air which would lead to increased storm intensity. Tune in to this weather station. We will keep you updated every hour on the hour."

I'd picked up a cup of coffee and sat in the car listening to the radio. Every hour on the hour? That should be enough to have lots of people, including myself, cross their fingers. I turned off the radio.

The Red Stick Farmers' Market was in full swing and I wasted twenty minutes browsing through stalls with vigorous looking vegetables. Then I walked up towards the State Capitol building to Spanish Town Road. According to my hastily assembled research courtesy of Google, it's the tallest state capitol in the United States begun by the infamous Huey P. Long and finished in 1932, two years before he was assassinated.

This neighborhood was supposedly a historic area with a true sense of community. It didn't look it. Trash was piling up at the curb, slats were missing in several fences, paint was peeling off gateposts. Not my idea of a historic area with community support. But what do I know.

Baronne Alley was not an actual alley but a small side street with a few trees. Number 3200 was right on the corner. The Big Ben bell chimed and its majestic strains echoed throughout the house when I pressed the button. That should bring results quickly. And it did. The door opened wide. Apparently crime here wasn't on anyone's mind. The woman in the doorway looked at me with her mouth open. Literally.

"You," she said and tried to close the door.

"Monique," I said equally astonished, stuck my foot past the threshold and pushed at the door with both hands.

"What's going on," a man's voice said from inside.

"I'm coming in," I said as Monique let go of the door and I stumbled inside.

"You," Jon Douglas said and brushed back his black hair with both hands.

"You'll both have to do a lot better than moan," I said.

"Oh," Monique moaned and went to a blue sofa in the bay window.

I swept past Jon Douglas and looked down at Monique.

"Where's Brandy Gregory?" I said.

"I don't know what you're talking about."

"Of course you do. Where is she?"

"I don't know and that's the truth."

"Fine. Then tell me who she is," I said.

"Brandy is my sister."

As simple as that. Monique's sister. Either Monique Jones was the former Monique Gregory. Or Brandy was married to a Gregory and they were both former something else. It always takes more effort to connect women both to their own former selves and to their sisters, aunts, grandmothers.

"And you're the former Monique Gregory?" I said.

"God, no. We're both Randalls. And Monique was Stevens before she married Gregory."

See, that's why a lot of us keep the last names we were born with. Simplifies your life not to mention skip-tracing.

"And you," I said to Jon. "What're you doing here?"

"Could ask the same thing. What are *you* doing following us around?" In daylight his eyes looked sea-green.

"She's a private investigator," Monique said. "Don't you know anything? Or you just so anxious to get in her pants that you forget where your head is?"

"You're a private investigator?" he said. "Why did you say you're a travel agent?"

"Because I'm both. And it's too long a story to explain right now."

"I'm leaving," he said.

"No, you're not," I said. "Not until we've cleared up a few things about Ricky Wilson and Brandy Gregory."

"Oh," Monique moaned.

"Stop that," I said.

"How did you find Brandy's house?" she said.

"She's an investigator, remember," Jon said.

"No, she's a snoop," Monique said.

What an irritating woman she was.

"Money is taken out of the account every month and I don't see Ricky using it," I said. "You have any ideas on the subject?"

"I have no ideas," Monique said. It's not easy to look innocent when you're so guilty. Monique both blushed and averted her eyes.

"Maybe you have an idea where your sister is?" I said.

Monique actually pouted.

"No, that's just it. She's not here. She hasn't called me since I can't remember when. No food in the kitchen. The cat was outside. Getting fed by the neighbor. No messages on her machine."

"And the money?"

"Don't know."

"Does she send you money every month?"

"Oh, okay, she does. Until I get on my feet."

Jon Douglas got up.

“I’m leaving,” he said. “I’ve already told you everything I know about Ricky. He’s been gone a long while. I don’t know where he is. I’ve never met Brandy. All I did was give Monique a lift over here ’cause her car’s on the blink.”

“Okay.”

“And I’m leaving,” Jon said again

“But how do I get back,” Monique wailed.

“I’ll take you,” I said. “I need to go over the house first.”

“You’re going to snoop through my sister’s house?”

“With your permission,” I said. “Or without.”

Jon stood at the door and looked at me.

“What about tonight,” he said.

“Raincheck,” I said.

“I’ll call you,” he said and left.

“He’s gotten to you, hasn’t he,” Monique said, “with his sweet music and his green eyes. You’d better watch out.”

I ignored her because it was half true.

The house was a small two-story with a living room, kitchen and half bath downstairs. Two bedrooms and a full bath upstairs. Not very neat, looked as if it hadn’t been cleaned in a while. There were dirty dishes in the sink and on the countertop as if Brandy had left in a hurry.

Monique turned on the TV and paid me no more attention. I could hear the weather forecaster going on about the Coriolis effect, tropical depressions, interactions with high and low pressure systems, the Yucatan Loop Current, and something about the eye of the hurricane named Katrina passing to the east of New Orleans.

The paperwork in the small desk in the living room was disorderly. Brandy had unpaid electric bills, unpaid mortgage statements, unpaid bills to a contractor who’d repaired the front steps, unpaid bills for the daily newspaper. But no bank statements. The next statement wasn’t due for another two weeks and according to Monique she hadn’t heard from Brandy for a week.

"When exactly did you talk to Brandy?" I had to shout to be heard over the TV.

"Couple of weeks ago."

"I thought you said a week ago."

"Well, two or three weeks ago. Don't remember exactly."

"When did she last send you money?"

"On August 2nd."

"She sent a check?"

"She sends money orders."

"And you talked to her after you received the money?"

"Don't think so. Can't remember."

"You're not helping," I said and she turned back to the TV.

I went upstairs and made a systematic search of the largest of the two bedrooms. The closet was jam-packed with out-dated clothing. Here was a pack rat who never threw anything away. Old down-trodden shoes lay helter-skelter on the floor. The top shelf didn't look any better. I dragged down a bunch of scarves, hats and belts. Impossible to know if she'd packed anything for a trip except I didn't see any suitcases. I up-ended the mattress. Nothing. I wasn't even sure what I was hoping to find.

The second bedroom looked neater. There was a man's shirt hanging in the closet but no other signs of a permanent occupant. Nothing under the mattress. The bed wasn't even made.

The bathroom had only women's make-up sitting in a disgusting heap on the counter. Brandy like Monique was not a neat-freak. Nothing in the cabinet under the sink.

I went back downstairs to Monique.

"Where'd you guess Brandy would go if she needed to get out of circulation for a while?" I said.

"She'd have come to me."

"You have no other family?"

"No one she's close to."

"Girlfriends. Boyfriend?"

"Ricky is her boyfriend."

"You think she left to be with him?"

"That'd be my guess."

"Did Brandy ever talk about taking a vacation somewhere?"

"Sure."

"Does she have a passport?"

"Don't need a passport to go to Vegas."

"You think she's gone to Vegas?"

"No, I don't. You need money to gamble. She ain't got no money."

"Let's go," I said. "I need to get back to New Orleans."

"What about lunch? I haven't had lunch."

I took her down to my favorite café, the Red Stick, where they were now serving lunch.

"We'll have the Gumbo," Monique said. "Bet you don't get a lot of that up north."

"Perfectly true," I said and tucked into the stew-like soup swimming with okra, peppers, shrimp, crab, and oysters on a bed of rice. Flavored with sassafras which gave the stew a deep red color. When I came up for air I had three cups of coffee.

"As good as it gets," Monique said and looked at me with watery eyes.

"When did you meet Doc Winnipeg?" I said and had to wait while she pondered her answer.

"About a year ago," she said.

"Where's he from? Doesn't speak like a New Orleans native."

She pondered again.

"No idea," she said.

"Where exactly does he live?"

"Oh, he's got a place," she said.

"With you?"

"What's it to you?" She got up.

"He must spend a lot of time in Haiti," I said and followed her outside. "Or does Antoinette do most of the work down there?"

"Why don't you ask *her*," Monique said. "And why don't you find Ricky instead of sticking your nose into my private life?"

"Somehow I have a feeling the two go together," I said.

Chapter 39

New Orleans, August 20, 2005

"The storm center forming in the Caribbean is moving rapidly towards the Florida coast. According to the National Hurricane Center a storm surge is expected which, combined with heavy rainfalls, may make roads impassable and cause landslides. We will keep you updated on an hourly basis or as often as necessary."

I turned off the TV.

"Bob," I said when I got him on the phone. "Brandy Gregory is Monique's sister."

"Hot diggety."

"I found her at 3200 Baronne Alley in Baton Rouge. You got the number right in the wrong town."

"Not the first time."

"And not the last," I said.

"What did she say?"

"Nothing. She's gone," I said.

"Gone where?"

"She's gone to join her boyfriend, Ricky Wilson, according to Monique."

"And you believe her?"

"Possibly. They have money coming in every month. They can lie low."

"True."

"And Rowland Brown's death may have been an accident which *Southwestern Oil* wants to keep under wraps," I said.

"Don't see how they can manage that. Thought OSHA would automatically be involved."

"They claim his injury happened when he fell having his heart attack. They've promised the widow a tidy sum maybe in an effort to avoid a law suit."

"Whatever that may be, it's nothing to do with us anymore," Bob said.

"I know."

"But you can't help pursuing this as a sideline, is that it?"

"I was in Baton Rouge anyway," I said. "Couldn't help myself. But I'll put it on the back burner for now."

"I talked to Martin Cook late yesterday," Bob said. "He sends his greetings. He's uncovered a couple of interesting facts about Antoinette Bazile and her paramour Toussaint Leautaud."

"So, they're not married?"

"No, they're not married. She was born here to Haitian parents who came over some twenty-five years ago, probably illegally. She went to school here, moved back to Haiti three years ago and became involved with Doc Winnipeg's non-profit organization *Cliniques d'Haiti*."

"That's more or less what Monique told us," I said.

"Correct. Antoinette's the executive director and travels to Haiti several times a month. She returned to New Orleans last year and bought the house we saw. She doesn't seem to lack money. Apparently her voudou activity is more of a hobby."

"Martin is supposed to find the financial records of the organization. That should reveal the sources of their income and the salaries of their executives and staff," I said.

"It's not clear to me what *Cliniques d'Haiti* has to do with Ricky's disappearance?"

"Just a feeling. I'm checking up on everyone in the small circle of people Ricky hung out with."

"Fishing expeditions," Bob said.

"More or less."

"In any case," Bob said, "a few months ago Toussaint showed up in New Orleans and moved in with Antoinette. There's no record of him entering the country legally."

"And neither one has a criminal record?" I said.

"Not in this country. Haiti may be another story."

"Maybe Martin is not the right source for that information. How about the FBI? You got any friends left there?"

"Should be one or two. I'll look into it."

"Fine, let me know."

"What's your next move?"

"I need to find Brandy Gregory and I have not the faintest idea of how to go about it. Any suggestions?"

"At the moment, none."

"You're supposed to be the superior investigator."

"What, as opposed to your inferior investigator?"

"Something like that," I said. "Doesn't make me feel very happy. I'll call you."

Fifteen minutes later I'd retrieved the rental car from the Monteleone garage and set out on route 90 across the toll bridge and the Mississippi River towards the Westbank Expressway and the Bayou Swamp Reserve.

The narrow bridge leading down to the dock was free of traffic and an empty tourist bus stood in the parking lot next to an ancient black Studebaker. I parked next to it and walked up to the cabin where Pete Brogan had his small office. The bus driver was sitting on a bench outside with a soft drink and a doughnut. A good healthy snack.

"Hey," I said. "Guess Cap'n Pete is out with a group of tourists?"

"That's right. Bunch of women from Europe. Holland, I think. All gung-ho about the alligators."

"I bet. Any idea when they're due back?"

"Shouldn't be more than half an hour," he said and swilled some sugarwater.

"I'll wait," I said and sat down next to him.

"Name's Orville," he said. "Been driving Pete's groups five years now."

"Great," I said. "Let me guess. You're also a protector of the environment and work with Pete at *Citizens for Environmental Clean-Up, Now!*"

"Yes, ma'am."

"Then you must have been at the rally last night," I said.

"Yes, ma'am."

"Too bad it was broken up."

"Yes, ma'am. But only what we expected."

"Any idea who started the fight?"

"We've a good idea but I'd rather you talked to Pete about that. He may not want me to discuss it with a stranger."

"Okay, Orville, will do. I'll wait for Pete."

I got up from my seat next to Orville and wandered down towards the pier. I sat down on a wooden post and contemplated the bayou. This part was a small inlet just large enough for Pete's ferry boat, and one or two others, to turn around. Spanish moss hung from the trees on the banks and duckweed and water hyacinths covered the surface of the water. The air was stagnant and the heat on the increase. Just sitting still I had beads of sweat forming on my forehead.

The chug-chug of the ferry boat could be heard from afar. Probably another fifteen minutes away. I got up from my perch on the wooden post and moved to the edge of the pier. There were no alligators this close to people and traffic. Instead I got to watch a family of otters busily building a bridge across two tufts of grass on the bank. No accounting for wilderness savvy.

Ten minutes later the ferry eased into the inlet and sidled up to the pier. Pete Brogan let down the gangplank and a festive group of stylish women in straw hats and designer sunglasses disembarked in a boisterous mood speaking an, to me, unintelligible language. And I took four years of German and had been told that Dutch was a cousin language. Go figure.

Pete Brogan didn't look that surprised to see me. He'd probably thought of me the entire day knowing I'd show up and planning how to handle me.

I was about to put it to the test.

Chapter 40

"We meet again," I said.

"So we do," Pete Brogan, marine biologist and environmentalist, said. He busied himself dropping the ferry boat anchor into the small harbor and securing the boat to the pier with a sturdy rope.

The last two women in the happy tour group boarded the bus and they all hung out the windows and waved to Pete and sang something that sounded like Happy Birthday but was possibly their national anthem. Orville tooted the horn three times, turned the bus around and departed with a clatter in a black cloud of exhaust. Time for an oil change, Orville.

Pete Brogan walked along the pier wiping his hands on a non-too-clean rag. He looked tired. The lines in his face seemed deeper than I remembered from when we'd first met and his eyes were not quite as blue. He walked with a slight stoop that I didn't remember either.

"Long day?" I said.

"All the days are long."

"You've got many irons in the fire," I said. "Who started the fight last night?"

"We know who they were but it's not necessarily any of your business."

"That may be true or maybe not."

"You're looking for Ricky Wilson. I don't think he has anything to do with us. I've never met him. You're on the wrong track."

"I went to see Rowland Brown's widow in Baton Rouge yesterday," I said.

"Margie Brown? You went to see Margie Brown? Whatever for? And how do you know her?" Pete shook his head.

"Maybe it's nothing to do with me or with Ricky Wilson," I said. "I thought you might want to know that his death wasn't a heart attack, it was an accident the oil company wants hushed up. They've offered Margie money to avoid a law suit."

"I know," Pete said. "You didn't have to look her up. I've talked to her and advised her against making such a deal."

"Ah," I said for want of something more intelligent.

Pete shook his head again.

"I was wondering," I said, "what happened the day I had to rush Bob Makowski away to the emergency room and you had to deal with whoever came to pick up Brad Sorensen's body."

"Nothing happened except an ambulance came along, two paramedics took the body, and two other men in dark gray suits and black ties made me promise not to speak about the accident to anyone," Pete said.

"What happened to the boat?"

"They said to keep it."

"Do you have any idea to whom it belongs?"

"No, I don't. I fixed up the engine to get rid of the salt water."

"It's in working condition?"

"Absolutely. Nice little boat."

"Is that the one tied to the pier?" I pointed towards the very end of the dock where the small boat bobbed up and down and looked good as new.

"Yep, that's the one. Can't keep it, of course. Can't get it registered without papers to show where I got it."

"Bummer," I said.

"And who were the guys who gave it to me? I've been wondering," Pete said.

"They were FBI," I said. "Nothing sinister. Brad was here undercover, they didn't want to jeopardize the rest of the operation. Especially Ricky, wherever he is."

"You haven't heard from him, I gather," Pete said.

"No, we haven't. And another thing. I've been wondering about the strange coincidence of you taking us to the abandoned cabin and finding, first, the overturned motorboat and, then, Brad Sorensen's body."

"Come to my office," Pete Brogan said and led the way inside the small cabin. There were two rooms, one serving as the reception with a rack filled with brochures. The second had a desk with a telephone and a fax machine and a bookshelf crammed with books.

"Have a seat," Pete said.

I sat down in a black wicker chair with a bright yellow cushion and Pete sat in an old-fashioned wooden swivel chair behind the desk.

"I believe my life is in some danger," he said. "I thought perhaps the motorboats we heard that night were after me. I'm afraid I used your and Bob's inquiry to make some investigation of my own. I was puzzled when we found the upturned motorboat and very afraid when we found the body. I thought perhaps they had mistaken Brad Sorensen for me."

"Your life is in danger?" I said.

"Yes. For the past few months I've been getting threatening phone calls and I know I've been followed both in town and sometimes even by someone posing as part of some of my tour groups."

"Wouldn't be a gray Chevy with a fat man in sunglasses behind the wheel?"

"Yes." He looked at me with his faded blue eyes. Surprised. "You've seen it?"

"Started to follow me after I'd visited the oil rig with Frank Smith, the public relations person at *Southwestern Oil*," I said.

"You visited the oil rig and you know Frank Smith?"

"I'd been led down the garden path by some types that shall remain nameless and thought Ricky Wilson had been sent undercover to investigate criminal activities involving the oil company and your environmental group."

"What kind of criminal activities?"

"I was told that your organization was responsible for several deaths aboard oil rigs and that the FBI had been called in to investigate."

"What utter nonsense," Pete said and got up from his swivel chair. He tried to walk around in agitation but there wasn't enough room with me sitting in the wicker chair so he sat back down.

"Libelous allegation," he said. "I will not discuss it."

"Let me ask you a different question, then," I said.

"Sure."

"What's your connection to Doc Winnipeg?"

"You mean Hubert Huffnagel? Don't know why he insists on that silly Winnipeg name. He's paid his dues, no reason why he shouldn't use his own name."

"You know about that?" I said. "I'm amazed."

"Why? It's quite simple. Hubert and I went to LSU together and were friends before he went back home to Ohio. He got in some trouble there and when he'd done his time he called me and asked about possibilities down here."

"You set him up in practice?"

"He can't practice medicine anymore. I helped him get started with the *Cliniques d'Haiti* organization. He can help distribute medicines in Haiti as a layperson. Yet, he's knowledgeable as a medical man."

"And he's a member of *Citizens for Environmental Clean-Up, Now!*?" I said.

"No, but he sometimes attends rallies. Makes his blood run faster, he says."

"I bet. Made mine run faster last night."

Pete finally laughed.

"I'll tell Mother," he said. "She's a good friend of Monique's."

"They're friends? Last night I got the impression they'd never even met."

"Mother doesn't wear her heart on her sleeve."

"*I'll* say."

"Monica, or as she calls herself now that she's the blues singer and voudou queen, Monique, was Hubert's nurse in Ohio. She also goes back to LSU, that's where we all met."

"And they're married?"

"No, Monica married someone called Jones. They just recently divorced."

"So she and the Doc don't live together?"

Pete laughed.

"It's hard to tell," he said.

"And how did Doc Winnipeg meet Antoinette?" I said.

"I believe he met her in Haiti. She runs his organization with a great deal of skill. And, of course, she knows Haiti better than anyone."

"And her boyfriend is Haitian. What does he do here?"

"I do not know."

"I get the impression that Antoinette's not a favorite of Monique's?"

"Ah, I don't get involved in their convoluted relationships," Pete Brogan said.

"Don't blame you. They seem to compete in the voudou department."

"I don't go in for it," he said. "And now, if you'll excuse me, I'm going to town to a meeting and then back home to Mother."

We walked together to the parking lot where he got into his Studebaker and I started up my rental car.

I waved to him as we drove off and he waved back.

Monique's story had turned out to be a lot more interesting than she'd let on at the Red Stick Café in Baton Rouge.

Chapter 41

New Orleans, August 21, 2005

"I want you to come home," Topsy said.

"You're calling me at six in the morning to tell me that?"

I yawned loud and heartfelt.

"I needed your undivided attention."

"You got it," I said and yawned again.

"Are you alone?"

"Of course I'm alone. And don't say it."

"I wasn't going to mention the name Jon Douglas."

"Thank you." I yawned for the third time.

"Have you been watching the weather reports?" Topsy said.

"Of course I have."

"I want you to come home. You'll get caught in some frightful tornado or hurricane or tropical storm, whatever it is they're having."

"It's a tropical cyclone also known as a hurricane and chances are it'll either dissipate if the ocean cools off or it'll make landfall somewhere else."

"You sound like a weather person. How do you know all this?"

"You know me, I pick up information by osmosis."

"Osmosis, my foot." Topsy said. "It looks bad to me. You shouldn't be roaming around in hurricane country."

"It always looks worse from a distance. It's not even raining here."

I slid down on my pillow and aimed the remote at the TV.

"I'm watching it as we speak," I said.

"The tropical storm system forming over Cuba and Bermuda has shifted in the last twenty-four hours," a cheerful weather forecaster said and swept her hand across a Doppler radar map. The blue and white swirling mass of the hurricane spun around crazily on the screen with no discernible direction. "Hurricane Katrina is rapidly gaining strength but it is too soon to predict exactly where landfall will occur. Stay tuned to this weather station for periodic updates."

"They say they don't know where the hurricane will make landfall," I said and turned off the TV.

"I don't care. If there's even the slightest chance you'll be caught in it you should leave."

"How's this? I'll leave by the 29th no matter how the investigation goes. You may make me a reservation right now if that'll set your mind at ease."

"And don't think I won't," Topsy said.

"What else is new on the home front?" I said.

"Ellie is back at work, thank God, her sister has recovered and Ellie has taken over the office again. She's terrorizing everyone."

"And how's your house search coming along?"

"I've found a darling house in Chevy Chase, red brick Georgian, small back yard, three bedrooms, walking distance to the Metro, what do you think?"

"Take it, take it."

"We need to sell the house in Virginia simultaneously. Bit of a tricky situation."

"Jack making trouble?"

"No, no. He's feeling so guilty he's bending over backwards."

"Better strike while the iron is hot. The longer you wait the faster the guilt will fade and he'll get tough."

"My, you're good. That's what my lawyer says."

"I'll lend you the money if you want to buy before selling in Virginia."

"I know and I appreciate it."

"Just say when."

Topsy stopped talking and I knew she was wiping her eyes. I've known her so long that I can see her face over the phone lines.

"And what's going on at your end?" she said after a while.

"Ah, what's going on at my end," I said. "I'm getting nowhere fast. It's a long story which I'll be glad to tell you at a future more convenient hour."

"But what's going on? I talked to Bob Makowski yesterday and he's going home with his leg in a cast today. He wouldn't tell me anything either."

"I've visited an oil rig," I said.

"An oil rig?"

"You're speaking to an expert on semisubmersibles, mud tanks, and motion compressor systems."

"You mean you went out on the ocean. The ocean which is brewing up a hurricane?"

"You've got a one track mind. Not a wind was stirring."

"I'm still worried."

"Okay," I said and swung my legs out of bed. "I gotta get going, thanks for calling, make that reservation if it'll make you feel better, and I'll be in touch."

"You're hanging up?"

"You'll see me before you know it. Ta-ta, Topsy."

"Goodbye," Topsy said with her nose in the air. I could see her clearly.

I turned the TV back on and got a different weather forecaster on the screen. This one was an analyst.

"If the eye of Hurricane Katrina passes to the east of New Orleans the wind would come back from the north forcing large volumes of water from Lake Pontchartrain against the levees and possibly into the city. It is estimated that this storm surge would produce waves reaching seven feet. We will be back with more coverage in half an hour."

I turned off the TV and went up to the fitness room on the top floor of the hotel. Thinking about the levees down at Jon Douglas' house near 17th Street.

While I was on the treadmill Pete Brogan had left a message on the hotel answering machine but I didn't notice the red light blinking until several hours later.

"I've been shot," Pete said.

Chapter 42

Pete had a large bandage covering his left temple.

We were at the Po'Boy Café way out of the tourist loop on the other side of Canal Street. Pete had a beer and I had chicory-laced café-au-lait. We each had, what else, a Po'Boy sandwich. Enormously large slices of French bread filled with shrimp and oysters and curly lettuce. Power lunch.

"What happened?" I said.

"I was in my boat. Someone took a shot at me. Just grazed me. Got myself to the emergency room."

"You reported this to the police?"

"Sure. And I mentioned the phone calls. Another one was left on the machine at the cabin."

"Recognize the voice?"

"No, no. All muffled like the other times."

"What are the police going to do about it?"

Pete drew slowly on his beer.

"You know. They said that there wasn't much they could do about it."

"No great comfort. What did the person say exactly?"

"Actually said that I'd better stay away from you."

"From me?"

"That's right."

I put down what was left of my Po'Boy sandwich.

"Must be someone who's seen us together in the last few days."

"That would be an awful lot of people."

"Was it a man's voice or a woman's?"

"See, that was hard to tell. Sounded like someone speaking through a filter."

"And yet," I said, "here you are being seen with me in public?"

Pete had a laugh that began way down in his stomach and worked its way up slowly.

"Thought you'd be the best person to talk this over with seeing you're an investigator. What do you think of the situation?"

"Not much."

"Take a guess, please."

"Let's see. Your rally was broken up the other night. Any idea where that came from?"

"*Southwestern.*"

"That's what I figured. And who would be sending threatening phone calls?"

"*Southwestern.*"

"What do they want from you?"

"Want me to stop writing to senators in Washington. Want me to stop talking to the press. Want me to go away."

"And you can't do that."

"No, I can't do that."

"Anyone else in your group getting phone calls?"

"No, I seem to be the only one."

We had some more beer and some more coffee. Never had so much coffee without it being decaf. The withdrawal symptoms would set in when I got back to routine in Washington. For now I'd have to keep the adrenaline flowing.

I stirred in sugar to keep the balance between a sugar high and a caffeine boost and was still stirring when Frank Smith came out of nowhere and hovered above our table. His meager hair was windblown and his ski-jump nose was red at the tip.

"Frank Smith," was all I managed to say.

"Surprise," he said. "And how is Miss Ruth Harcourt, free-lance journalist? Or, silly me, is it Miss Jamie Prescott, private investigator, today?"

It was either the recent infusion of caffeine or the sugar high or the unmasking of my evil ways. I felt light-headed.

"Which one do you know, Brogan? Which one has she pretended to be for you? Or maybe you don't care. One fraud's as good as the other to you?"

"Hey," Pete Brogan said. "You're talking about a lady."

"She's no lady," Smith said.

"That's true," I said.

"Long's you're here," Pete said, "you should know the police are aware of the harassment you're subjecting me to."

"Blow it out your ass, Brogan," Smith said.

"Watch your manners," I said.

The tip of Frank Smith's nose reddened further.

"Patty Underwood is very upset with you," he said to me.

I had no problem looking embarrassed. I decided on the path of least resistance. I kept my mouth shut. Had put enough feet in it already.

Pete Brogan finished his beer in one long gulp and waved to the waitress. I swallowed some coffee but left half of it behind when I stood up.

"You'd better watch out," Frank Smith said to my back but I heard him quite clearly. "Or you'll end up in a place you don't even want to think about."

Pete Brogan and I walked out together and Frank Smith left right behind us. He walked to the curb and got into a fancy looking car with tinted windows and we watched him disappear.

"Ruth Harcourt, free-lance journalist?" Pete said and smiled. "What was that all about?"

"A failed mission to snoop on the oil industry," I said. "Ruth Harcourt has retired."

"How did he find out about you?"

"I'm surrounded by blabbermouths," I said.

"And sometimes you go overboard?"

"Now why would you say that?"

His smile got wider.

"And I wonder if that's your phone ringing at the bottom of your bag?" he said.

"Should keep it in my pocket," I said and fished it out.

"Hello?"

"Martin Cook here, how are you?"

"Good. Must be important for you to call my backpack," I said. "What's up?"

"Just got a report about your Haitian man, Toussaint Leautaud. Detained yesterday at Miami International Airport trying to explain away his false passport."

"You know someone in Miami," I said. It was more of a statement than a question.

"I was with Immigration, remember, before I branched out," Martin said. "I've still got my contacts and I had a quiet feeler out in Miami. Friend of mine kept his eyes open. When this came up he called me."

"How did they identify him? I thought he had no criminal record here?"

"Ah, but in Haiti he does and they matched his fingerprints there."

"He got sent back right away?"

"Didn't waste any time. Less expensive than feeding him here in detention. Wonder how long before he's back."

"Not long, I'm sure. Nice work, though," I said although it wasn't clear how this information would help me find Ricky Wilson. But as I always say maybe a big fish will bite while I trawl for the smaller ones.

Pete looked at his watch.

"There's something I have to check out. And I need to get back to the ferry. Got a tour scheduled for two o'clock."

"The Dutch women coming back?"

He laughed.

"Swedish," he said. "They were Swedish."

"And they're coming back?"

"No, it's a high school group from Wisconsin."

"I want you to report to the police again," I said. "Can't hurt. It's their role to keep the citizens safe."

"And you'll see what you can find out?"

"Absolutely. And watch your back in the meantime."

"You, too," Pete said.

Chapter 43

Jake's Jazz Club was in full swing at nine. Jake was at the bar. He pointed me to a stool and signaled for me to wait a second. The *Jon Douglas Stompers* had heated up the room. People were rocking, a few got up and gyrated between the tables.

I'd told Jon I'd meet him there at ten after his last session. For a drink, no dancing. Although I supposed we could always take a lap around Jake's floor.

"What'll it be tonight, sweetie," Jake said.

"How 'bout a Hurricane?"

"Coming up, but better not joke about it. We're planning to board up the windows tomorrow. Just in case."

"You know something I don't?"

"Been here twenty years. Got wise."

The Hurricane arrived in a tall glass with a straw and a fancy slice of blood orange. It was sweet with dark rum and passionfruit juice and could last me at least an hour. Jake put a plate of crawfish next to the Hurricane and winked at me.

"Mudbugs on the house," he said. "Waiting for someone?"

I nodded and he winked again. How did he know? Or maybe he didn't know I was meeting Jon. I slouched down behind the back of the guy next to me. He was swiveling on his barstool in sync with the music.

At nine-thirty Jon stepped off the stage and let his trio continue playing without him. He came towards the bar and I was about to get up when he stopped at a table for two and sat down.

The woman leaned forward and said something to him and he laughed. She had on a strapless top and I could see the folds of her red skirt under the table. Her arms and shoulders were suntanned. She had a glass waiting for Jon and he drank deeply and stuffed something in his mouth from a plate on the table.

They leaned their heads close together and started talking. I could see the woman's face but only Jon's back. She had Brooke Shields eyebrows, a good nose and pouty lips. Red. Once in a while Jon smoothed down his black hair behind his ears and sipped from his glass. But somehow it looked as if he never stopped looking at her face or listen intently to what she was saying. At one point he leaned back in his chair and laughed. It was infuriating.

At a quarter to ten Jon reached into his pocket and pulled out something which he gave to her. She slipped it into her purse. Looked like a key to me.

Jake came around and removed the almost empty platter of crayfish and gave me another Hurricane. While he was doing that the woman got up and left as if suddenly in a hurry. When she passed me I saw she had bare feet in high heels with thin straps and bright red toenails. She didn't look back at Jon and he didn't look back at her.

I swivelled around.

"Brandy Gregory?" I called out.

She stopped and pointed to herself.

"You talking to me?"

"Are you Brandy?" I repeated.

"Sorry, honey. You got me confused with someone else," she said and went out the door.

"Her name's Donna," Jake said.

"You know her?"

"Not really. Just happened to hear her name."

I finished my drink.

Jon had joined his *Stompers* and finished the session playing one more Coltrane piece. He dipped the sax with eyes closed and leaned his entire body into it. His black hair fell into his eyes. He warbled the last notes up and down the scale, lowered the sax slowly and opened his eyes. The room was silent before the applause erupted. When his players left he walked casually to the bar and sat down next to me.

"Hey," he said. "You're here already. Didn't see you come in."

"What're you drinking?" I said and waved to Jake.

"Nothing right now. Maybe a little later."

Of course, he'd already had his fill.

He smoothed back his hair and looked at my face, at my lips, at my hair. He leaned close and put his hand on my arm. He smiled when I shivered and ran his fingers down to my hand.

"You look good," he said. "Your nose is back in joint."

"So is yours."

"What else is new?" he said and smiled his detestable smile, the one he'd bestowed so generously on the slut in the red skirt and matching toenails.

"Let's see. What's new?" I said. "You haven't run into Ricky by any chance?"

"Not that again," he said and took back his hot hand. "He'll come back when he's good and ready and not before. He's that kind of a guy."

"Is he?"

"Yes, he is."

"And you know him that well?"

"Better than you seem to," he said.

He had a point. I didn't know Ricky Wilson at all. I only knew his face from a photo which could just as well have been of Brad Sorensen. A forgettable face. A man everyone wanted me to forget about.

Jake switched channels on the TV and a new weather person came on with a serious face. Seemed that Hurricane Katrina had turned around and was picking up strength and might become a Category 3 hurricane by the time it reached the coast. A spokesperson for the National Hurricane Center was interviewed and expressed concern. The weather forecaster warned that oil production in the Gulf might be shut down unless the storm by-passed the coast.

"I'm definitely boarding up tomorrow," Jake said. He changed the channel to football and everyone went back to their drinks.

"I'll be going to Los Angeles on the 1st," Jon said. "Big gig. And then back to Washington. My season starts September 15. How about you? When are you going back?"

"I have reservations for the 29th."

"With or without Ricky Wilson?"

"With or without."

Jon looked at his watch and got up.

"I'd invite you back to my place for pizza and cold beer," he said. "The refrigerator is working again. Cost me a bundle."

"But?"

"But I'm all tuckered out. Been a long day."

"It must have been," I said.

"How about tomorrow instead? I finish at ten as usual. The night will still be young."

"Let me see how it goes," I said. "I'll call you."

At least I got the last word.

Chapter 44

"What do you mean," Topsy said. "He left you for a woman with sprouting eyebrows?"

"Looks like it. This isn't turning out much better than the blind dates you set me up with."

"Sorry."

"Me, too."

"I got your reservation for the 29th. You'll be home by the evening. Write down this number."

"Thank you," I said and wrote it down.

"I'm buying the house in Chevy Chase," she said.

"Need the money now?"

"Thank you, sweetie, but Jack is advancing it unless we sell the house in Virginia in time."

"He's being very amenable."

"He's trying to be a gentleman, he says."

"A bit late for that."

"For the sake of the children, he says. Doesn't want to lose their esteem."

"And yours? Is he going to restore *your* esteem?"

"Maybe."

"Isn't it too late for that. Still seeing his bimbo?"

"Oh, Jamie, she's not a bimbo, she's a lawyer. I'm just a housewife."

"Excuse me? You're just a housewife? Thought that expression went out when Betty Friedan came in."

"You know what I mean."

"No, I don't know what you mean. You are a successful businesswoman. You run our travel agency almost single-handedly. You have a master's degree in English literature. You write a column in a national magazine. You're the Grammar Guardian. You keep hundreds of thousands of readers on the grammatical straight and narrow."

It's true. Even in high school Topsy was a relentless stickler for the correct usage of English grammar. By the time we reached college her dexterity on the subject made English professors blush at their grammatical slips and made her fellow students—myself included—think twice before speaking. No one would be caught dead confusing laying down with lying down. Or say "between you and I," instead of "between you and me," utter redundancies such as "return back" and "separate out," or confuse advice with advise, affect with effect, capital with capitol.

"Jack's lawyer bimbo has nothing on you," I said with conviction.

"She has Jack," Topsy said.

"And you want him back?"

"Not anymore. Because of her."

"Or because of Jack."

"Oh, whatever."

The waiter brought in my late supper and looked around for a place to set the tray.

"On the floor?" he said.

"You remembered."

"Who was that," Topsy said.

"Room service with turtle soup, oysters Rockefeller, and bread pudding with whiskey sauce."

"You can eat all that this late?"

"It's not that much. The soup plate is small, there are only six oysters, and the bread pudding is tiny."

"You're lucky nothing sticks to your ribs."

"I exercise, remember."

"My exercise consist of running up and down the stairs and walking back and forth to the Metro."

"You're a lazy bum."

"Not so much."

"Listen," I said. "I have an idea. Why don't you join my professional women's de luxe tour to Paris, Vienna and Budapest? Ellie will manage on her own and you need a vacation."

"Thanks but no thanks. I'll wait for the professional men's de luxe tour."

"Just a thought," I said. "Will you do me a favor?"

"Name it and you got it."

"Call Martin Cook, my Internet sleuth, first thing in the morning, his number is on a card on my desk. Set up a meeting with him at his office on K Street."

"What's the meeting about?"

"He'll give you an envelope with some paperwork. I want you to take the envelope to Bob Makowski tomorrow."

"And why can't Martin Cook take the envelope directly to Bob. Or FedEx it over?"

"Because Martin hates Bob and I need it done tomorrow. No time for FedEx. And you ask too many questions."

"Okay, I'll do it. I have to be downtown anyway. Consider it done."

"Goodnight, Topsy."

"Or as good as it'll get," she said.

It was past midnight but I called Bob anyway.

"Did I wake you?"

"Why would you think that. It's only twelve-thirty."

"Topsy is coming over tomorrow afternoon with the financial statements for Doc Winnipeg's non-profit organization."

"How did she get them?"

"Martin got them."

"And why isn't he bringing them over himself?"

"I told Topsy Martin hates you and that's why I need her help."

"You're nuts, you know that. If you're trying to set her up on a date with Martin there must be an easier way."

"It's an emergency. She needs some manly attention right away."

"Women," Bob said and hung up.

I ate the turtle soup and downed the oysters. Then I left a message on Martin's office machine telling him to invite my colleague, Topsy Bannister, out to lunch tomorrow—accepting no excuses—and to give her the envelope with Doc Winnipeg's financial reports to give to Bob Makowski. If she questioned why he couldn't do it himself just say, Bob hates me. I finished the bread pudding.

Suppressing the urge to watch another hurricane forecast I left the TV alone and went to sleep.

Chapter 45

"Small groups by appointment only," Antoinette's website said. And then there was a lot about her powers and her spiritual calling being superior to those of all others who were only pale imitations of her, the Priestess Antoinette. And to please make donations to support this important work.

Ridiculous and devious all in one go.

The Yellow Book had several pages of travel agencies and it took me the better part of an hour to find the right place.

"What I really want," I said to Betty Bartlett, owner of Bartlett Travel in the French Quarter, after introducing myself as the owner of Prescott Travel in Bethesda, Maryland, "is a very private tour to the voudou temple of Priestess Antoinette."

"You mean a tour for one?" Betty said.

"Precisely. I'm a devotee of voudou and would like exclusive access to her."

"We usually take a minimum of three and a maximum of five."

"I will, of course, pay you for a maximum of five," I said. Easy to be generous on an expense account. "How fast can you arrange the tour?"

"Let me call Antoinette. I'll get back to you shortly."

"No need to mention I'll be the only tour member," I said. "She might refuse since she's used to at least five people buying stuff."

"Not to worry. I'm sure you'll buy enough stuff for five," Betty said. And she didn't even know about the expense account.

Ten minutes later Betty called me back.

"We're all set," she said. "Meet me in half an hour and we'll walk over to Antoinette's."

"Don't know how to thank you," I said.

"I must say I can't wait to meet you."

"Likewise," I said. "I'm on my way."

Bartlett Travel was in a good location on Royal Street near the corner of Dumaine squeezed in between an antique store selling French furniture and *objets d'arts* and a hat shop featuring frilly concoctions. Bartlett Travel's window display had a plastic alligator baring two rows of teeth and carrying a sign advertising tours of the bayou.

Betty was a tiny woman with gray curls and sparkling blue eyes. She greeted me at the door and looked up to my towering height.

"My, you're tall," she said.

"Can't deny it," I said.

I get that remark quite a lot. Never understood why. It wouldn't occur to me to say to someone, my, you're short.

"And I'm short," Betty said. "We're like Mutt and Jeff."

"Okay."

"We're two blocks away from Antoinette's."

"Can't thank you enough," I said and tried to shorten my steps to match hers. It still worked out to three of hers to one of mine.

"I'm a voudou afficionado myself," Betty said. "It's wonderful in this day and age to know someone will protect you and give you comfort. The Temple is a place of tranquility and spirituality."

"You're not a Catholic, then?" I said.

"Oh, yes. For more formal occasions."

"Of course."

“They don’t have women pristesses,” Betty said. “They should. It’s more comforting.”

“Ah,” I said in the absence of a more enlightened reply. Topsy would have been better at this. Always open to utterances of the weird.

“I love the Juju bags. They protect me from negativity and evil.”

“Juju bags?”

“Yes, you know, *gris-gris* bags. *Gris* is French for gray. It’s spelled with an s, but you pronounce it “gree.” You must get one. Hang it above your door. Antoinette will anoint it for you with a special oil.”

“Okay.”

“But never open it or the magic will spill out and the wrong influences will enter. You should also have a horseshoe above your door and a mirror above your stove, a little good luck Buddha and a lucky penny.”

I struggled for something to say.

“Isn’t the mirror a Feng Shui thing?” I said.

“Yes, exactly. I see you’re knowledgeable. You must also clean your front steps with red brick dust to protect the entrance to your house or business.”

“Red brick dust?”

“Yes, it will keep negative people away from you. It’s an ancient New Orleans remedy. A favorite of the esteemed Marie Laveau.”

“Ah, Marie Laveau,” I said.

“The Mother of us all,” Betty said.

Topsy really should have been here. She’ll try anything. And red brick dust on the doorstep to Prescott Travel might keep away those tiresome travelers who insist on perfect service and found luggage.

We entered through the front door to Antoinette’s temple. The small museum-cum-shop had no windows or if it did, they were covered. Oil burned in several lamps hanging from the ceiling and the floor was strewn with oriental rugs placed across and under each other as stumbling blocks. The shelves were filled with more potion oils, herbal blends, incense burners, voudou dolls, candles, books, videos, Haitian art, and posters than I remembered from my first visit.

"She brings in the most valuable potions from Haiti," Betty whispered. "The love potions are especially precious. Not that I need them, of course. I'm married."

"My dear Antoinette," she said in the same breath. "I'm here with your exclusive tour."

Antoinette stood near the wall and blended in perfectly with the hangings. As regal as the first time I saw her. She looked beyond me for the other tour members. She looked at Betty. And then she gave *me* the evil eye.

"Hoooo," she whistled softly and I could feel the negative forces rush towards me.

Betty laughed nervously.

"Betty, this is an undesirable visitor," Antoinette said. "She is not welcome. You need to leave."

"I don't understand." Betty sounded tearful. "She will buy enough for five."

"It's not a matter of money. She has an evil effect on me. Her vibrations contaminate the temple."

"Betty," I said. "Sorry to have dragged you into this. I'll buy a few things, you'll get your commission, and we'll leave."

I grabbed a couple of *gris-gris* bags in red flannel tied with black string, selected some potions and lotions, some faceless dolls, and a variety of candles.

Under the watchful eye of Betty Antoinette rang up my purchases and threw everything into a bag with the imprint "Have a Nice Day."

"I'll need a receipt," I said thinking of my expense account.

Antoinette handed me the receipt just as the front door opened.

Doc Winnipeg was on the stoop. His hair stood on end and he was dressed like an undertaker in a black suit and a black tie.

He didn't see me.

"Look what I brought you," he shouted. "The bloody fool came back in. He'll be the ruin of us all."

Toussaint didn't look as if he would be pulling off any chicken heads today. He was dressed in dirty sweats and muddy sneakers. As if he'd recently climbed a fence and fallen into a riverbed.

"Brought you everything you need," he said and dumped a backpack on the floor.

"Doc, we have company," Antoinette said.

He peered into the darkness behind her.

Once he'd recovered at the sight of me Doc Winnipeg didn't look amused. He brushed right past me into the middle of the shop.

"What's she doing here?" he said.

"Snooping," Antoinette said.

"Getting tired of you," he said to me. "If you're still looking for Ricky Wilson stop coming to us for answers. I don't know where he went and who he really was. I'll ask you as nicely as I know how: Get the hell out of our lives."

He opened the door and showed me out. Betty fluttered out behind me.

"That was putting it nicely," I said

Chapter 46

"Listen," I said to Bob. "Things are getting murky here."

"I'm listening."

"Doc Winnipeg and Antoinette have something going and Slim-Jim Toussaint is involved. I can't figure it out."

We had a lengthy pause during which we each chewed on that. Nothing to digest so I moved on to the next subject.

"Toussaint tried to get in on a fake passport, was caught by Immigration in Miami, and was sent back to Haiti without being detained."

"Wish they were always this expeditious. Save the taxpayers a lot of money."

"Not really. He came back if not the very same day then the next."

"How?"

"My guess is over a fence on the Mexican border."

"Or walked across somewhere without a fence."

"Exactly."

"How do you know?"

"Intelligent deduction."

"No, really."

"I happened to be on a one woman exclusive voudou tour of Antoinette's temple."

"How did she let you in? I thought she didn't like you."

"A lovely travel agent by the name of Betty Bartlett—a sometime Catholic devoted to the comforting rituals of voudou—got me the tour."

"Under false pretenses."

"Under false pretenses and we basically got thrown out. But I got her a hefty commission on the stuff I bought. Chargeable to my expense account."

"And will you give Gwen Wilson the stuff you bought?"

"Will she appreciate a *gris-gris* bag? Or a voudou doll without a face?"

"You know what, I think she might. She has Feng Shui mirrors all over her apartment."

"Are you sure you two are compatible?" I said.

"In most ways."

"Aha." I swallowed my tongue. "Anyway, Doc Winnipeg showed up with Toussaint at Antoinette's just as I was winding up my shopping spree."

"You have all the luck."

"Toussaint dumped a backpack containing who knows what at Antoinette's feet and said he brought her everything she needed."

"Any thoughts about what that might be?"

"I have a few. Then Doc Winnipeg lectured me about Ricky and told me to get the hell out of everyone's life."

"Aren't you yearning for the day when everyone will love you?" Bob said.

"I should be so lucky."

"Don't seem to be getting any closer to Ricky," Bob said. "Maybe give it a rest, come home, we'll regroup."

"Not quite yet. Still have a few things to check out."

"Gwen is pestering me about the hurricane season and says she can't be responsible for keeping you down there."

"I wish everyone would stop worrying about hurricanes," I said. "They come and go, or so they tell me, and we'll have enough warning if it gets really desperate."

"You promise you'll leave in time?"

"Topsy has me on a flight to Washington on the 29th. Happy?"

"Happy."

"I talked to Pete Brogan," I said. "He's receiving threatening phone calls and someone took a pot-shot at him."

"Think your pal Frank Smith is involved?"

"It crossed my mind."

"He's not happy with you," Bob said.

"Did you tell Patricia Underwood my real name?"

"Wild dogs couldn't drag it out of me."

"She's a hyena."

"She didn't get your name from me."

"Frank Smith knew," I said. "He assaulted me at a Po'Boy café while I was chewing away on a world class sandwich."

"I'm having cereal for lunch," Bob said.

"Send out for Chinese."

"I'll wait for Gwen."

"Pete let slip that Monique was Winnipeg's nurse in Ohio."

"Interesting. Could've been involved with the scam. Didn't get charged, though."

"She married someone by the name of Jones, divorced him and returned to New Orleans with Doc."

"Intricate relationships. Just goes to show you that the only normal people are the ones you don't know very well."

"But what good does all this do us?"

"Wait and see, wait and see. Things have a way of falling into place. Let's try to think outside the box."

"Thank you, professor."

With that advice in mind I snapped on my money-belt which contains all my vital papers, grabbed my brown wig and granny glasses, and returned to Antoinette's place.

Chapter 47

Finding parking in the French Quarter requires substantial luck and some hutzpa. Since I'm never in want of the latter, I squeezed my rental Ford into a space meant for a Mini-Cooper.

I put on my wig and glasses and walked the short block to Antoinette's where I settled against a wall, behind a tree, across the street, and prepared to wait on an empty stomach. Not even coffee.

The lights were on in the house but the porch lay in darkness. The windows were open and I could see people moving around behind the curtains but no one came down the steps. After half an hour of self-imposed inactivity I crossed the street and tip-toed into the garden by-passing the stairs to the porch.

Doc Winnipeg's muffled voice came through but I couldn't catch any specific words. Antoinette shouted something that sounded like '*a bas*'and Toussaint answered. I crept closer, found a wooden crate and stood up so I could look inside.

Before I could see anything Antoinette's voice sounded close to my face.

"I'm ready," she said.

I ducked, fell off the crate and stifled a cry just as the window was slammed shut. Antoinette went around to the rest of the windows and closed those, too. I crouched down just below the steps to the porch but when I was illuminated from above by the porch lights I had no choice but to roll away on the ground until I ended up underneath and joined a myriad of spiderwebs.

Dust and gravel rained down from above as heavy feet shambled across the porch and down the stairs.

"I don't like the place," Antoinette said.

"Believe me, it's the best," Doc Winnipeg said.

"I still think you should do something about it," she said.

"Okay, okay."

I held my nose and suppressed a sneeze. It took them several minutes to disappear down the alley to the street and when they were gone I succumbed to the sneezing while I crawled out and brushed off the dust. When the light on the porch went out I hurried to the street.

They had piled their luggage into a green hatchback parked to the right of the entrance. Antoinette was at the wheel with Doc Winnipeg in the passenger seat. I waited just long enough for the car to start up before I eased out of the alley and, hugging the wall, sprinted towards my car.

I fender-bent my way out of my tight parking spot and caught up with the green hatchback as it rounded the first corner. From then on in it was easy going. They were on their way to the airport.

I stayed right behind them all the way to the parking area, found a space about ten cars from theirs and followed them at a safe distance behind several people wheeling suitcases. I stopped at a Dunkin' Donuts stand behind a huge woman who shouldn't have been ordering an extra large Dunkachino with whipped cream and three glazed donuts. I asked for a Cappuccino with skim milk and kept an eye on my prey. They went straight to American Airlines and checked in bound for Haiti.

I turned around and looked as they went to the line forming at the security check-point. They took off their shoes and placed some items in the gray plastic bins. They went through without being questioned.

At the hotel I called Bob Makowski and left a message. Then I called the American embassy in Port-au-Prince and was put right through to Walter J. Hood, III, U.S. ambassador to Haiti.

Chapter 48

Port-au-Prince, Haiti, August 22, 2005

The Port-au-Prince International Airport teemed with assorted tourists, a few returning Haitians, greeting relatives, men in uniforms with guns on their hips, and porters wheeling luggage to an uncertain destination.

Don't take a cab, the ambassador had said on the phone, my driver will pick you up. I had the strap of my carry-on around my shoulders, my money-belt strapped to my waist, and felt pretty much on top of things. In the old days I would've rented a car or jumped in a cab, but that was then and this was now. A small group of men in camouflage pants and black tees had come menacingly close the minute I walked out of customs and would-be cab drivers walked in step with me offering cheap fares.

The embassy driver was right outside the exit in a black limo with tinted windows and an armed guard in the passenger seat.

"Miss Prescott?" he said.

"Absolutely," I answered and jumped into the back. I felt tension mount as we swung away from the curb and narrowly missed another small group of guys in army fatigues who'd loitered around the hood of the car.

We moved rapidly south from the airport towards Petionville but it wasn't long before the car was slowed down by traffic. The tap-tap mini-buses—completely covered with faded voudou-inspired decor and looking more run down than I remembered—disgorged and loaded on passengers at every other corner.

Tall peasant women walked along balancing baskets with fruits and vegetables on their heads. A single donkey with a withered old woman slumped on its back stumbled along with bent head. Notwithstanding political and economic upheavals the poor plodded on with their sad lives.

The residence of the U.S. Ambassador to Haiti was a large modern house on Rue Villatte. Only the roof was visible behind a tall wall with broken glass imbedded on top. This was softened by a profusion of bougainvilleas.

We were buzzed inside, an armed guard secured the gate, and I was greeted by Jill Hood standing in the doorway.

"What a lovely surprise," she said. "Come in, come in. Walter will join us in a moment."

Jill Hood had brought her furniture and her eclectic decorating expertise with her from Chevy Chase. The house was filled with Japanese vases, Hungarian folk art, and Indian brassware.

"I still don't believe it," Jill said when we were seated in the large living room on matching white sofas. She poured coffee into tiny Chinese cups from a silver pot.

"Here we are twenty-two years later and not a day older," Walter Hood said and slid his hand across his bald pate.

Jill and I had come to Haiti as wide-eyed exchange program volunteers. For six exhilarating months we spent our days in Croix des Bouquets filling in as first grade teachers, our weekends at Kyona or Ibo Beach, and our nights partying in Petionville and Kenscoff with Embassy staff in general and Jill with military attaché, Walter J. Hood, III., in particular. Jill and Walt married the following year and went off on assignments to such diverse spots as India and Budapest and Japan. The last time I had dinner at their house in Chevy Chase was just before their posting to Haiti half a year ago.

"Never thought we'd end up here together again," Walter said and cast me an enigmatic look. "You were rather cryptic on the phone. What gives?"

"I'm here to pick your brains," I said.

"You've always been good at that," Jill said. "You lead such an exciting life."

"And I thought you were the one with the glamorous existence," I said.

"Not so that you'd notice," she said. "Circumstances have changed here for the worse. Not a day goes by without kidnappings, death threats, murders, and armed robberies. If you're planning to walk in the streets better take off your jewelry. And don't go to the bank to change money. Someone will be on the lookout for you around the corner and attack you. And they usually work in groups of three or four."

"Are these the erstwhile Tonton Macoutes?"

"Probably some of them," Walter said. "When you realize that one in ten men in Haiti used to be Duvalier Macoutes allowed to terrorize the public, kill and rob and bribe, it would be naive to think they'd all become law-abiding citizens. There would be no profit in that."

"I'm shocked at everything that went on back then," I said. "Any idea what happened to Madame Max Adolphe?"

"Who was she?" Jill said.

"She was the Supreme Head of the Tontons Macoutes under both Duvaliers. Supervised torture and killings of thousands. A monster of a woman. I heard she made a deal in 1986 when Baby Doc fled and that she escaped to the States. Probably with a different name. Dropped out of sight completely. Should have been tried for crimes against humanity."

"Oh, God," Jill said. "That's obscene."

"It went on right under our noses," I said. "I'm mortified to think we were so clueless."

"No one talked about it," Jill said.

"We hung out with the wrong people."

"You mean the elite, the good guys?"

"If that's not an oxymoron," I said.

"You were young," Walter said. "And you weren't involved in politics."

But he hadn't been young, I thought. He had known exactly what was going on. He was still in the know. I felt a small chill run down the back of my neck.

"Tell me," Walter said, "what are you investigating and how can I help?"

I decided to backtrack.

"I didn't mean I'm actually investigating anything," I said. "This is partly a vacation and partly an attempt to find an old friend."

"Bet I know who it is," Jill said. "But is that really a good idea? He stayed on here and married you know who, and she watches his every step like a snake."

"No, no, no," I said. "That was hot when it was hot and it was over when it was over. I'm looking for an American woman by the name of Antoinette Bazile."

"If she's an American I'll check if she's registered with the Embassy. That's what we recommend for all Americans. That way we can warn them of any emergency situation. They cannot count on help from the local police," Walter said. "I'll be right back."

"Bad, isn't it?" I said after he'd left the room.

"You have no idea," Jill said. "Embassy children under 21 are not allowed to live here with their families, or even to visit. The twins are 18, they'll be on their own at Yale during the school year and go to my parents when vacation starts."

"I knew it was bad, but not this bad," I said.

"No one of that name registered with the Embassy," Walter said when he came back. "And can't we have a good-sized mug of coffee instead of those pathetic demi-tasses?"

"That would be good," I said.

"Oh, all right, we'll have it in the den," Jill said.

"Next coffee-break," Walter said. "I'm on my way to the office. Jamie, why don't you come with me. You can tell me the details on the way and I'll assign someone to help you."

"Bring her back in one piece," Jill said and to me she added, "You're staying with us. I insist."

I'd actually imagined myself lounging in solitary comfort at the Montana Hotel further up the mountain, taking some time off at the pool, drinking rum punches at the bar under a palm-thatched roof, and eating quiet breakfasts in the dining room overlooking the mountain side. But I could tell it was not to be.

The Embassy on Boulevard Harry Truman felt like a fortress but reassuringly safe. I'd given Walter a vague story about Antoinette, the friend I'd lost touch with. I'd omitted any mention of Ricky Wilson, the involvement of the FBI and about finding Brad Sorensen in the bayou. I wasn't sure if Walter would mention my kind of visit in his weekly report to Washington but I didn't want to raise red flags. In fact, I cursed myself for having called him in the first place.

"And how are you planning to go about your search?" Walter said as we swung in through the gates to the embassy.

"I'll start with the phone books," I said.

"And you will call everyone by the last name of Bazile?" Walter laughed. "Bound to be a couple of hundred. I'm assigning our second secretary, Donald Levine, to you. He's been here a while and knows his way around."

Don was in his fifties, a thin, wiry guy with dark eyes and black hair. Looked more like a teacher of English as a second language than a second secretary. But what do I know of diplomats.

Chapter 49

"Not too difficult," Don Levine said when I'd explained that I needed to find an Antoinette Bazile most likely in Port-au-Prince.

"I have an address of sorts," I said. "A post office box number in Port-au-Prince. I've written but never got a reply. Thought I'd look her up in person as long as I'm here."

"Main post office," he said. "Then we're in business. Give me half an hour and please don't ask me how I do these things."

"You have friends in high places," I said.

"Or in low places."

"My kind of man," I said.

I gave him an hour during which I read the Miami Herald, The New York Times, and the Wall Street Journal in the ambassador's front office. When Don returned he looked sweaty as if he'd been running a mile.

"The physical address listed for the post office box is 920 Rue du Centre," Don said. "The owner is Antoinette Auberge Bazile listed care of *Cliniques d'Haiti*. Does that sound like the party you're looking for?"

"It certainly does. And I can't thank you enough," I said hoping he wouldn't ask me about *Cliniques d'Haiti*.

"What's *Cliniques d'Haiti*?" he asked.

"I have no idea," I lied. "Maybe Export-Import? Women's cosmetics? I'll ask her when I see her."

"Rue du Centre is near the Iron Market, walking distance from here. I'll be glad to go with you."

"I can find it," I said. "Don't want to take up any more of your time."

"You sure?"

"I'm sure.

Don handed me a cell phone and a card with his phone number.

"Here," he said. "The ambassador wants you to have this phone. You can return it to him when you leave. He says he's sure your's isn't working here."

"And he's absolutely right," I said. "Tell him thanks."

The temperature outside was in the high 80s and I pulled my wide-brimmed hat well down over my eyes. I had no intention of walking by Antoinette's house on Rue du Centre in broad daylight looking white and blonde and tall and American. Instead, I headed for the Iron Market just for the fun of it. But I never got that far. When I came to the end of the street my borrowed cell phone rang.

"Hey, Jamie," Walter said. "Any results yet?"

"Don located my friend's house and I'm on my way over there," I said.

"Glad Don could help. Listen, something's come up and I'm very apologetic and so is Jill but I've just been informed of an impromptu visit by a congressman and his party. They're arriving from the Dominican Republic this afternoon. I'm afraid they expect to be put up at our residence in Petionville and we only have so many bedrooms."

"No problem," I said almost too brightly. "Maybe I'll stay at the Montana."

"Don't roam around," Walter said. "I can have you chauffeured to the Montana whenever you're ready to return to Petionville."

"I'll see you in a bit," I said and turned around in my tracks and headed to the Oloffson, the hotel everyone knows thanks to Graham Greene's novel *The Comedians*, although he called it the *Trianon* and placed it in Petionville. It's still old, still a wonderful gingerbread mansion and the food is still excellent despite the endemic ups-and-downs in the country. I walked through the lush garden with its palm trees and bougainvilleas and sculptures and sat on the latticed veranda at a round table with a white tablecloth.

After lunch I went inside and secured what they said was their last room, and I half believed them. I also rented a car to be delivered within the hour. Hitching rides in ambassadorial limos doesn't suit me. I like my independence. Then I phoned Jill.

"What a disappointment," she said. "Instead of you I get a congressional party. Do plan on staying with us as soon as the junket from Washington leaves."

"For sure," I said hoping my insincerity didn't show. "But listen, I've decided to stay at the Oloffson rather than at the Montana. Always wanted to experience that famous ambiance up close and personal."

"Oh," Jill said. "Oh, I'm so envious. Sounds wonderful. You'll meet all kinds of fabulous people. They all hang out at the Oloffson. Or so I hear. The driver will deliver your bag within an hour, how's that?"

My bag arrived exactly as Jill had promised at the very moment my room was ready for occupancy.

Chapter 50

Port-au-Prince, August 23, 2005

The house was a small brick building with a partly chipped enameled sign with the number 920 in black on dirty white. The wooden door had a metal knocker with a brass ring. I parked my rental car around the corner and walked slowly by the house.

Rue du Centre was a busy road and I had no trouble looking like a tourist, leaning against a wall, watching the scenery. Not right across from number 920 but close enough. Someone behind me tugged at my sleeve and I looked down at the leathery face of an ancient woman with a pipe clamped between her sunken lips. She held out her hand and I dropped a *Gourde* into it. She took the money, ironed out the crumpled paper with her fist and stuffed it inside her blouse.

The door of number 920 opened and a tall skinny Haitian stepped outside. He walked away briskly without looking either to his left or to his right.

"*Gros Negre*," my ancient woman whined. "*Gros Negre Vaudou Houngan*."

"*Quoi*?" I said and bent down to make out what else she was mumbling. But she quickly slumped further down against the wall, closed her eyes, and went to sleep keeping her hands clutched around her tattered blouse.

I moved away and stepped into a small stationery store where I bought a newspaper. From there I saw Antoinette come out from number 920 carrying several baskets. She locked the front door and looked up and down the street before she walked briskly towards the Iron Market. Looked like we were doing an early morning food shopping.

I let her get well in front of me before I crossed the street and followed her. The tall gray and orange painted iron structure stretched around an entire city block. The food stalls started on the sidewalks outside of the market proper. Tables were piled high with vegetables and some with dead chickens laid out on their naked backs.

The stagnant air was malodorous, the smell of urine rather sickening. People were sleeping near the walls on dirty sacking next to enameled plates with the remains of chicken bones. Some scabby dogs lay there with half-open eyes filled with pus.

I pushed my way inside the marketplace past tables heaped with used clothing, tee shirts turned inside out, and frayed jeans. Antoinette had stopped at a stand with several crates of fruit on the floor and was arguing with the peasant woman, presumably about the price.

When her baskets were full she returned to the house on Rue du Centre. It was nearly noon and I went further down the street on the other side. My withered woman had disappeared and had left behind a pile of soiled newspapers.

A car pulled up at the house with Doc Winnipeg at the wheel. Antoinette came out as if on cue and got in the car next to him. They sped away.

I waited five minutes before I crossed the street with my lockpicks at the ready.

Chapter 51

It was a new lock made—as most things in Haiti—in the U.S. It caused me no grief at all. My main concern now was whether anyone was still in the house. I stood in a small foyer with closed doors, one on my right, one on my left, a stairway going up, and a kitchen at the end of a narrow passageway straight ahead. The silence hummed in my ears.

I went to the door on my left and turned the knob very carefully. The lock snapped open and I let the door sit ajar a moment before I peered inside. It was a small parlor with overstuffed furniture and a threadbare rug on the floor. The window shutters were closed and the room felt hot. There was no one there.

The door on the right led into a larger room with bay windows. There was a desk against the wall and several upholstered chairs around a table on a pedestal foot. I walked to the desk and riffled through a small pile of newspapers, some photographs of Haitian children, and a stack of pamphlets advertising *Cliniques d'Haiti*.

The desk drawer was open as if someone had removed the contents and hadn't bothered to close it. The file drawer contained the paperwork. Not much of a filing system. Just two large envelopes stuffed to capacity. I scooped them up and pulled out a couple of pages. A letterhead with an unfamiliar name. Couple of invoices. Scribbled notes. I crammed the envelopes into my small backpack before returning to the passageway.

The stairs creaked at every single step. I tried to tiptoe up close to the wall but the old wood creaked anyway. The small landing at the top of the stairs had three closed doors which I figured to be two bedrooms and a bath. The bathroom was very small. The first bedroom had one double bed, a bedside table with a lamp and a small dresser. The second bedroom had an old lady sleeping under a canopy in a large bed.

Her lips quivered in her sleep, her hands fluttered across the bedcover. I got a whiff of sickness when I pulled the door shut. And that's when I heard the key in the door downstairs and Antoinette's voice in the foyer. And, a moment later, hurried steps coming up the stairs.

I had no choice. I fled into the second bedroom.

Behind the door was a French armoire. I opened the double doors and found it was empty. It would do as a last minute hiding place although I didn't relish the thought of sitting helpless at the bottom of a closet.

Antoinette shouted down the stairs.

"She's sleeping. Come help me. Get the bags. I'll be ready in a second."

The door to the bathroom opened and shut, water flushed, another door opened and closed, steps came up the stairs, doors kept opening and closing. There was a scuffle as something heavy bumped against the walls, exclamations and a single shriek and, then, silence.

I went to the window. Doc Winnipeg, his light hair plastered to his skull by the humidity, was loading a hefty bundle into the back seat of a car parked at the curb. He straightened up, lifted his head, and stared up at my window—or maybe at the window next to mine. Whatever it was, it made me take a step back and bump into the only chair in the room so I missed seeing what he did next.

When I came back to the window Antoinette was getting into the driver's seat, and I had a fleeting glimpse of Doc Winnipeg next to her before the car sped away.

The game was over. They were headed for the airport and I'd better get out of the house. There were no sounds from downstairs so I took the stairs five steps at a time. I reached the foyer just as the key was turned and the door opened. I scooted in behind it and stood against the wall. I heaved in a deep Tae Kwon Do breath.

The man closed the door and turned around. It was the *gros Negre,* the *gros Negre Voudou Houngan.* He wasn't that large, actually, and came only to my shoulder. The whites of his eyes popped in panic when he saw me. I had the advantage of surprise but the disadvantage of being up against a wall. No room to maneuver with side kicks or back kicks or anything else fancy.

He dropped the bag he was carrying and reached for his gun. He fumbled and couldn't get it out before I took one step forward and used the best short-range weapon I possess. My elbow. I clipped it across his jaw, grabbed his arm, twisted him around and got behind his back. I dug my fingers into the pressure points at the inside of his elbow and forced him down. He sprawled and moaned into the floorboards, while I stepped over his body and stumbled out the door. He didn't recover enough to follow me.

The rental car chugged along ominously but recovered its spirit by the time I hit the highway to the airport. I didn't expect to see Doc Winnipeg's car, and I didn't. When I turned into the parking lot at the departure hall I was surrounded by a pack of kids with their hands outstretched. I distributed enough *Gourdes* to ensure they wouldn't vandalize my car and walked inside. The hall was empty and I realized the morning flights had come and gone.

Back outside I walked to the fence surrounding the field. Doc Winnipeg and Antoinette were walking behind a porter towards a snazzy Learjet. The porter carried a large bundle up the steps and disappeared inside. Then the Doc and Antoinette boarded carrying their own bags.

The plane taxied out to the runway and took off.

Chapter 52

Back at the Oloffson I put the two envelopes from Antoinette's desk in my duffelbag, locked it, and stowed it away in the closet. I'd examine the contents later.

My computer now had very little battery time left, just enough for me to find a list of clinics and hospitals in Port-au-Prince most of them with addresses. I picked the nearest one on Rue Pavee and within fifteen minutes stood in front of an old building set back from the sidewalk. Street vendors and market women competed for space. Dogs and children roamed around. The smell from the gutter was hard on the nose.

The main door opened right into a large room with several desks and with people—mostly Haitian—walking around. There was no reception area and I stood inside the door trying to decide whom to approach. A thin American-looking man with gray hair and sunken cheeks standing at a file cabinet seemed to be the best choice.

"Hi," I said. "Have a minute?"

"Sure," he said without looking up from the file drawer.

"I'm looking for a clinic with mobile medical units called *Cliniques d'Haiti* which is run by a charitable organization out of New Orleans."

"Yeah?" At last he looked up at me. "Plenty of clinics here and plenty of charitable organizations."

"And you know most of the organizations operating in Haiti?"

"Most, but probably not all."

"Did you ever run into a Doctor Winnipeg?"

"Winnipeg, Winnipeg," he said. "You know, somehow the name rings a bell but I really can't place it."

"Try," I said.

"What? I'm sorry but you'll have to excuse me. I must finish up here, don't want to spend my time doing office work. I'm off to Cap Haitien."

"They have offices at 920 Rue du Centre," I said. "Sure you haven't run across them?"

He dropped his paperwork into a battered briefcase and looked at me.

"Where do they operate?" he said.

"All over, apparently," I said and showed him the *Cliniques d'Haiti* brochure.

He looked at the photographs and scanned the written text.

"Looks good," he said. "But I haven't run across them."

"Does the name Antoinette Bazile sound familiar?"

"Haitian name," he said. "But not someone I know."

He picked up his briefcase and headed for the door.

"Thanks for your time," I said and gave him my card. "I'm returning to the States, would you call me collect if you think of anything?"

"Glad to," he said. "But don't hold your breath."

He left me with a nod that was not unfriendly, just that of a man in a hurry.

When I got back to the Oloffson I cut through the veranda and found Don Levine sitting at a table near the entrance. Not the person I needed right now. I wanted to get my bag and head for the airport. The next flight left in three hours.

"Join me for a drink," he said and pulled out a chair.

"Could we do this later?" I said.

"Nothing like the present."

"Okay. Just one drink," I said and sat down.

"What'll it be?"

"Rum punch, please," I said. It arrived with extraordinary speed and I took a big gulp.

"I've been waiting for you," he said. "I made some inquiries at the consulate. Seems your friend Antoinette Bazile left Haiti early this afternoon with her mother. Her mother has obtained a visitor's visa on humanitarian grounds to receive medical treatment in the States."

I stared at Don Levine probably a bit too long while I digested the information and thought of the woman in the bed at 920 Rue du Centre. I hadn't checked her room before I left the house. Did they take her downstairs and into the car? I thought of the commotion on the stairs and the bundle in the back of the car. Was she lying down on the seat? Had the porter carried her aboard the Learjet? It was just possible.

"That's disappointing," I said and swallowed the rest of my rum punch. "Sorry to have missed Antoinette."

"Guess that ends your search," he said.

"It does," I said and put down my glass. "I'll be leaving this afternoon."

"Good. The ambassador will be glad to hear that," Don said.

"Really? Why?"

"Doesn't think this is a safe place for you. And I agree."

Don Levine held out his hand.

"Better give me back my cell phone," he said.

I produced the phone.

"I'll tell the ambassador goodbye for you," he said.

"I'll give him a call," I said.

"He won't be available," Don said.

He stuffed the phone in his pocket and stood up to leave. He looked at me as if he was on the verge of adding something but thought better of it. I didn't get up and I didn't exactly say goodbye.

I called Jill Hood from the local phone in my room. The message I got was that Mme. Ambassador was occupied and could not come to the phone. Sounded all around like the end of a beautiful friendship.

I went to collect my gear. The door to the closet stood slightly ajar. I yanked it open but I already knew what I'd find. Or wouldn't find. My duffelbag was gone.

Chapter 53

New Orleans, August 24, 2005

"What do you mean you've been to Haiti," Bob said.

"Just for a couple of days," I said. "And it wasn't any fun at all."

"Spill it."

"Happened to know the ambassador. You've met them. Jill and Walter Hood. They've been in Haiti six months."

"You stayed with them?"

"I was invited but my luck changed due to a congressional junket from Washington and I went to the Oloffson."

"And?"

"Walter lent me his second secretary for the duration."

"Why not his first?"

"Very funny."

"What did you find out?"

"Don Levine found Antoinette's street address for me."

"Wait a minute," Bob said. "Don Levine? Short guy, too much black hair?"

"You know him?"

"Didn't know he was in Haiti," Bob said. "Special agent. Old friend of mine."

"Aren't they all," I said. "And he was assigned to me? Weird coincidence."

"Maybe no one else was available?"

"Don't think so. He stole my duffelbag from my hotel room."

"You left your bag in a Haitian hotel room?"

"I thought the papers would be safer there than on my back roaming around town."

"What papers?"

"The ones I found in Antoinette and Doc Winnipeg's house."

I could hear the moaning at Bob's end of the line.

"You're sure Don Levine stole your bag? Could it have been someone else? An ordinary thief?"

"It crossed my mind. In which case my Calvin Kleins are on sale at the Iron Market as we speak. Slim pickings, though. My valuables were strapped to my midriff. But I think it was Don. He seemed very anxious for me to leave."

"Maybe he doesn't like blondes?"

"I think he does, but we weren't dating."

"Why would he be stealing your bag? Did he know you had been to Antoinette's house and had taken papers out?" Bob said.

"Could have seen me. Or it could have been a routine search. Or speculation. We'll never know."

"Or maybe we will."

"But what do you think of this: The Doc and Antoinette left Haiti in a private Learjet. Your Don Levine said they were taking Antoinette's mother to the States for medical treatment."

"And I imagine you're following up on that?"

"Absolutely. But, hello, what's this. Turn on your TV. I'll get back to you later."

I hung up the phone and watched the news flash in disbelief.

"Breaking news," the newscaster said. "A report has just come in that Peter Brogan is dead."

A large photo of Pete was at the top of the screen and I looked into his kind eyes and could almost hear his deep laugh.

The laugh I'd heard only a couple of days ago. How was this possible. Where did he go when we parted? He'd said he had to take care of something. What was it? Why hadn't I probed further? Too many terrible questions. I moaned. I felt a pain stirring deep in my chest.

The announcer looked straight at me and I pointed the remote at her and turned up the volume.

"Peter Brogan is dead. He was only fifty-two," the announcer said. "It was with special sorrow we at this news station received the report early this morning. Pete has been a guest on this program untold times over the years and we knew him well."

The announcer looked down on a piece of paper getting her next sentence together. Her voice was hushed.

"Marine biologist, former professor at Tulane University, prominent environmentalist, founder and president of *Citizens for Environmental Clean-Up, Now!* defender of Louisiana's disappearing wetlands. He was found dead last night of an apparent heart attack aboard his boat at the Swampland Reserve. He is survived by his wife, Yvette Brogan. He had no children."

The announcer had three people in the studio sitting across from her, all looking solemn.

"It was a shock," the first man said. "Peter Brogan was an upright, decent, committed man who would never give up when fighting for what he thought was right. His work with the organization was outstanding. He was responsible for stopping some of the acts of vandalism in the wetlands. He will be sorely missed."

The announcer turned to the only woman on the panel who looked close to tears.

"Pete was fighting the big guys in the oil industry," she said and looked defiantly into the camera. It zoomed in closer on her face. She didn't flinch but kept staring. "He put his whole life into the fight. He wrote repeatedly to senators and representatives in Washington to sound the warning bells. He appeared before Congress to testify about the deterioration of our wetlands. But it was an uneven match against a powerful lobby. And now that he's gone we must continue that battle without him."

The announcer turned to the third man. He had on rimless glasses and a severe suit and tie. He looked around trying to see someone off camera and his eyes flickered here and there. Hadn't been properly prepped. Didn't know where the cameras were.

"Yes, it was a shock," he said and looked to his right.

The camera quickly panned away from his face but he kept on talking.

"Peter Brogan fought hard but didn't always know when to say when. He was so obsessed with his cause that he went overboard especially when it came to the oil companies."

He paused and looked to his left. The cameraman had a hard time knowing what he was going to do.

"Unfortunately," he said, "Pete was influenced by people who didn't know the facts, or who didn't want to know the facts, about the great work the oil companies are doing to protect the environment. I know of many people who would have liked a rapprochement but Pete was a stubborn man and it didn't happen. That said, Peter Brogan will be sorely missed as the great human being he was."

Trust the media to go for a balanced picture.

While the last man spoke I dialed Bob.

"I'm watching it," he said. "It's on the early news. NBC."

"I've got to leave in a few minutes," I said. "Just needed to touch base again."

"Seems Pete was well known in Washington. They're having people on the news saying what a great guy he was and how much he did for the environment."

"Anyone from Louisiana?"

"No, Patty Underwood must be out of town. But Ted Kennedy is talking about Pete right now. Calling him an American hero."

"Imagine that we'd never heard of him. Thought he was a ferry boat operator. I feel humbled."

"What do you think," Bob said.

"I'm thinking what you're thinking."

"That this might not be what they're saying."

"Can hardly cover up an accident if that's what it was," I said. "Or could they? Rowland Brown comes to mind."

"Too many deaths," Bob said. "Looks like a cluster to me."

The newscast switched to an update on the weather. It was now firmly established that Hurricane Katrina was heading towards the Gulf Coast. They were still talking about the Loop Current. The hope was that the hurricane could cease to have tropical characteristics if it was deprived of the warm water that fueled its strength.

"The last thing Pete said to me two days ago was that he had to go take care of something," I said.

"Or maybe he meant he was meeting someone?" Bob said.

"Possibly. Look, I want to get down to the dock and see if I can find Yvette."

"Be careful."

"Okay."

The *Picayune-Times* was on the floor outside my door. It had a large picture of Pete—a much younger Pete in a suit and a tie loosely knotted—on the front page with a three column headline. And an editorial on the second page. I tucked the paper under my arm and went down to the garage.

When I came out through the exit to the street the gray Chevy with the large man in sunglasses got busy starting up. But instead of following me he made a U-turn on the narrow street and lumbered away. If he knew I recognized him he obviously didn't care. I made a serious note to find out who he was. He had followed Pete Brogan. But could *Southwestern Oil* really be that incompetent?

Chapter 54

I was back on Route 90 like a pro, going over the toll bridge across the Mississippi River towards the Westbank Expressway. I saw the sign to the Bayou Swamp Reserve at the last possible moment. When I got off on the exit ramp the gray Chevy was there again. Right behind me. Maybe not such an amateur after all. I wondered what he'd do when we got to the narrow bridge leading to Pete's cabin and the pier. He'd be very obvious there.

I needn't have wondered. When I got to the dirt road just before the bridge he stopped, made one of his laborious U-turns and disappeared. I decided not to worry about him.

A silver Honda was parked in the lot behind the cabin but no one was in it. I walked up to the cabin and opened the door. The reception room smelled of mildew.

"May I help you?" The woman stood at a small desk sorting out a box of papers. More boxes were stacked on the floor. She was in her early fifties dressed in a white skirt, a yellow tee, and canvas shoes. She'd been crying.

"My name is Jamie Prescott," I said. "I was a recent friend of Pete Brogan's."

"He mentioned you," she said. "My name is Meg Patton. I helped Pete out down here a couple of times a week. I came down early today to sort through some of his papers."

"I'm wondering where I can find Yvette," I said.

"She went back to their cabin in the bayou late last night."

"Was she with him when he had his heart attack?"

"No. Orville, his bus driver, found him at seven last night. There was nothing he could do."

"Did Orville know when it happened?"

"He couldn't know that," Meg said.

I guess he could have if he tried to take Pete's pulse. Or tried to revive him.

"Orville was in shock," Meg said. "He called an ambulance and waited for them to arrive."

"And did the paramedics say when it might have happened?"

"No," Meg said. "I don't think it matters."

"Did Orville call Yvette?"

"They have no cell phone reception out in the bayou. He took the small motorboat Pete found last week. Pete was going to turn it in to the police 'cause the hull identification number had been removed and it was probably a stolen boat. But he never got to it. A good thing, too, or else Orville couldn't have gone out to tell Yvette. He can't maneuver the ferry boat."

"And is the motorboat still at the dock."

"Yes. Yvette came here in her own boat and Orville drove her to the hospital."

"And she returned home in her own boat?"

"Yes, of course." Meg looked as if she couldn't believe how dense I was.

"Meg, did Pete tell you I was helping him with an investigation?"

"No." She looked astonished. "An investigation? Into what?"

"Can't really tell you," I said. "Pete wouldn't have wanted me to talk about it."

"No. No, of course not."

"Do you have the key to the small motorboat?" I said.

"It's hanging over there on the wall behind the door."

“Does the boat have enough fuel?”

“I know Pete filled it up. But then Orville took it back and forth. Don’t know how much is left. But there’s a pump out back.”

“I’ll be right back,” I said.

“Where are you going?”

“To check out the boat.”

“You’re taking it out? Do you know how? Are you licensed?” Meg was suddenly all professional energy.

Even if I hadn’t been licensed, so what? As it happened I have a license from Maryland and it would have to do. Not that a license means that much when in some states the minimum age for a motorboat operator is twelve.

“Yes, I’m licensed,” I said. “I need to see Yvette.”

“You’re taking the boat out?” she said again.

“That’s the idea.”

“If you’re really going could you take this envelope and give it to Yvette. It’s Pete’s life insurance policy. She never asked for it but she’ll need it.”

“Sure thing,” I said. “Anything else she’ll need from here?”

“One moment,” Meg said and went into Pete’s office. She came back out with his backpack and his captain’s cap. The one he’d worn to impress the tourists. It was white with a black visor.

“Don’t know what’s in the backpack,” she said. “But he always took it with him on the ferry boat. Yvette should have it.”

“You have a navigation map of the bayou?” I said.

“A map? No, I don’t. Pete didn’t need one. He knew the bayou like no one else.” She struggled with the tears.

“Have you been out there much?” I asked. “Could you make me a rough picture so that I don’t take the wrong turn?”

“Sure. It happens to be rather easy.” Meg got a pen and a piece of paper and made a square for the dock and two squiggly lines for the channel leading into open water.

"Once you're in open water you keep going until you get to the first fork." She drew in the fork.

"Bear left and keep going until you get to another fork." She drew in another fork.

"Bear left again and keep going. You'll see the pier ten, fifteen minutes later. On your left."

"How long should it take me?"

"About forty minutes."

I got the key down from a nail on the wall and picked up the backpack and Pete's cap.

I waved to Meg and she waved back. I walked down to the pier. The boat looked a lot smaller than I remembered.

Chapter 55

The rope was in a knot that loosened readily enough. I tossed it into the boat and jumped in after it. The boat was still damp inside. The floor boards had warped and mold was beginning to form along the edges. I checked the sides for leaks and found none. I placed Pete's backpack, his cap, and the envelope with his life insurance in the cockpit under the wheel and turned the key.

Nothing happened.

I turned the key again and the engine growled. Reluctantly. Just thinking about it until it decided to purr and rumble into action.

My cell phone rang. Probably the last call before I went out of range on the water. The screen said "Private Caller."

"Yes," I said and began steering the boat away from the pier.

"What's that noise? I can hardly hear you."

"Who's this?"

"Jon Douglas."

"Ah, Jon Douglas," I said and speeded up.

"Can you hear me?" he shouted.

"You'll have to speak up."

"Jake called me last night and said that you'd come to the Club early," Jon shouted.

"And?"

"He says you saw me with my sister."

"Your sister? Isn't 'cousin' the accepted euphemism?"

"No." And he laughed or more like chuckled. "My honest-to-God older sister, Donna. Came from Florida for one night. I had to spend the rest of the evening with her."

"Look, I don't know why you need to tell me that."

"Don't you?"

"No, why?"

"Because I don't want any misunderstandings between us. *I fancy you* as the Brits say."

The boat sputtered and coughed. I slowed her down and swung around slowly.

"Did you hear me?" Jon said. "I don't want to lose sight of you."

"You won't," I said.

"Good. Where are you? What's the noise?"

I steered the boat into the middle of the channel towards open water.

"I'm in a boat," I said. "I'll catch up with you later. I'm losing the connection."

Water sprayed in my face and it felt as good as when I'm setting out from Annapolis on a Saturday afternoon cruise on the Chesapeake Bay. Except for the heat and the Spanish moss and the alligators and the racoons and the water hyacinths.

There never seemed to be any traffic here. The land on both sides of the waterway was solid ground rooted by trees and covered with grass and flowers I'd never heard of. Together it formed a dense underbrush until the land suddenly dropped under the water level and became swamp. Here the water hyacinths were staying close to the banks. Hard to see where swamp ended and solid land began.

It was a mysterious and quite wonderful environment. The one Pete had preached was disappearing. That had been the crux of Pete's struggle. That the oil companies had used the channels for shipping and prevented the build-up of the Delta by natural deposition of silt. That the earth around the edges of the canals erode as a result and that salty water seeps in and kills the vegetation that's needed to secure the land.

My boat puttered along with a few splutters but Pete must have dried out the engine thoroughly. The fuel gauge was at three quarters and I lifted my face to the sun. The water was eerily motionless without any visible currents. The only movement I saw was the occasional water snake under the surface. The trees on the banks swayed in a persistent breeze and, on the banks, the inevitable unwieldy alligators sunned themselves in imperial and ancient majesty.

After ten minutes I got to the first fork in the water and steered left. The watercourse got narrower as it was separated into two and the Spanish moss hung closer overhead. I was still to meet or to hear another boat and there was no habitation on the banks. Who knew, maybe it wasn't solid land after all but marshy swamp. Maybe if I tried to walk on it I would sink. Seemed the alligators were keeping watch just in case.

After another ten minutes I got to the second fork in the bayou and steered left again as Meg had told me. The waterway got even narrower and treestumps and other debris in the water rattled against the hull of the boat. A couple of egrets fluttered up about my head. I remembered Pete's warning that silt would build up at the bottom and that I might get stuck. He had used a wooden pole to steer clear of the banks but I didn't have one. I tried to stay smack in the middle of the channel hoping it would widen. The channel did widen after another few minutes and I was back out in almost open water. Meg's little map said that I'd come upon Yvette's pier on the left-hand side after another ten minutes.

It didn't happen. After twenty minutes I knew that I was in the wrong channel. The watercourse opened up to many more forks. I took a left whenever that happened thinking I'd keep to the same direction. But it was impossible to know in which direction I was actually going. The bayou was spreading out and dividing up.

As Pete had said, the weather in bayou country was unpredictable. He'd said that even when nothing seems to be happening something happens. It was happening now. A struggle was forming between the air and the water. Clouds I hadn't seen a moment earlier now spun around in circles much like the Doppler had shown the tropical storm whirling in the Gulf. Raindrops began to pummel the water. The water was rising imperceptibly as if infused from below.

I steered the boat close to the nearest bank and slowed down. Two alligators left their looking posts and swam away. I could hear birds flutter and fly away. The moss hanging from the trees swayed in the wind. The water was coming down in droves whipping up the water and rocking the boat. I barely kept dry under the roof of the small cockpit.

It was over as quickly as it began. The clouds whirled away, the rain stopped. I steered the boat back out to the middle of the waterway and made a U-turn. At the next fork I took a right, and at the fork after that I took another right. That led me into a very narrow channel from which I hastily backed out. There were more forks in the bayou than you could shake a stick at. The wide channel that Yvette's pier would be in had disappeared. The humidity was rising. I was soaked through. There were no boats in sight.

The air was still as I steered the boat along.

Chapter 56

It got dark early.

I was lying on the narrow banquette next to the cockpit. My cell phone didn't work. The boat had no flares, no radio. It had no anchor, no bullhorn like the one Pete had on the ferry. If I'd been a smoker I'd have had matches to set something on fire.

The boat spun to the side and bumped into the bank. There were no trees close enough to the water for me to tie the rope. I had considered some of the Cypress knees sticking out of the shallow water but couldn't get close enough without the boat getting stuck.

Because I had finished the small bottle of water I'd carried onboard in my backpack I was thirsting for more. I can go with water an entire day but because I didn't have any I needed it desperately.

The night creatures were stirring. An owl hooted and another answered. The water rustled with nocturnal life. Fish came up snapping for air. I imagined the alligators were sleeping. The wind had died down and the rain had stopped.

I opened up Pete's backpack and found a stale sandwich in a brown paper bag and a thermos with black coffee. I ate the sandwich and drank the coffee but it wasn't as good as plain water would have been right now.

I put down the thermos and listened.

From very far away I heard the drone of an engine.

Someone was out there. I got up from the banquette and stood at the railing.

"Hellooooooo," I shouted. "Over heeeeere."

The droning came nearer and I shouted again.

The droning waned.

I looked around for something that would make a noise and picked up the metal thermos. I banged it on the metal railing and it made a pathetic little pling.

They would come back, I told myself.

I sat down on the banquette and leaned against the side of the boat. I dozed off. Vaguely I felt the boat rock, the wind howl, the rain come down. I struggled against a large weight before slipping under.

Circling in the void, floating silently. The bubble turned, trembled and sank into the rippling water staring fish-eyed into space. Clinging to the wet skin it somersaulted and stayed head down, hearing, not seeing. Something stung. Someone shouted. Someone moaned. The tunnel narrowed, the silvery globe in the dark blue square was a thin gleaming thread being sucked into nothingness. White lights blinked and gyrated. Rising up high the bubble floated once more before sagging into soft space.

Inside the bubble looking out.

Chapter 57

Bayou Country, August 25, 2005

"She doesn't have a pulse," the voice said.

Yes, I do, I shouted but I didn't hear my voice.

"Have you called the ambulance?"

"They're coming," the voice said.

"Is she dead?"

"Yes."

NO, I shouted. But I didn't hear my voice.

"How long had she been in the boat?" the voice said.

"Since yesterday. She left in the morning around nine."

"She got lost," the voice said.

Yes, I got lost, I shouted. But I didn't hear my voice.

"I don't understand it. She wasn't out there that long. And she wasn't in the water. What could have happened?"

"Who knows. Dehydration. Shock. A stroke."

I'm in shock, I shouted and tried to open my eyes. But my voice was silent.

"Here's the ambulance," the voice said.

"Where will they take her?"

"To the morgue."

"No," I shouted and I heard my voice. I opened my eyes and saw light.

"No," I whispered and someone took my hand.

A thousand voices spoke at once. They were too loud and I closed my eyes. When I looked up again I saw Meg Patton's face and she was smiling.

"You're all right," she said.

"We didn't think you'd made it," another voice said and I knew who it was.

He came into a blurry focus.

"Doc Winnipeg," I whispered. "How did you get here?"

"I came out here to visit with Yvette. To comfort her. Meg told me you had gone there but hadn't returned. I took the ferry out and found you unconscious."

"Thank you," I said.

"I was glad to help," Doc Winnipeg said.

The two paramedics asked me questions.

"Do you know your name?"

"Jamie Prescott."

"Where do you live?"

"In Bethesda."

"Do you remember what happened?"

They had brought out a chair from Pete's cabin and sat me in it. One of them placed an ice-pack on my forehead.

"I went out to visit Yvette," I said. "I got lost."

"What's the last thing you remember," Doc Winnipeg said.

"I heard a boat, I shouted for help, no one came. I fell asleep. That's all I remember."

"And that was sixteen hours ago," Doc Winnipeg said.

"We should take you in for a check-up," the paramedic said. "You look a bit wobbly to me."

"What about my car," I said.

"I'll get it to your hotel somehow," Meg said. "Not to worry. Just get better quickly."

I called Bob from the ambulance.

"I've been trying to reach you since yesterday," he said. "Where have you been?"

"I got lost," I said.

"What do you mean?"

"I got lost in the bayou," I said.

"And where are you now?"

"I'm here," I said. "I feel funny. Call you later."

The paramedic who sat next to the gurney reached over and wrapped a black cuff around my arm to take my blood pressure. He pumped it full of air until I thought my arm would fall off.

"Elevated blood pressure," he shouted to his buddy up front. "Let's step on it."

I heard the siren and felt the ambulance lurch. Then my cell phone rang and I couldn't get to it.

"Want me to answer that for you?" the paramedic said.

"What's your name?" I said.

"Tom."

"Yes, Tom, that would be nice," I said. "Please answer my cell phone."

I heard him tell someone that they were taking me to the emergency room at Tulane and I assumed that he was talking to Bob.

After that I didn't hear any more.

Chapter 58

New Orleans, August 26, 2005

"I'm back," I said.

"Are you at the Monteleone?"

"Came in half an hour ago."

"What did they say?"

"They said I'll live."

"What happened?" Bob said. "From the beginning."

"The boat we found near Brad Sorensen was stolen. No hull identification number."

"Yes, Pete told us."

"He was going to turn it in but, in the meantime, I used it to visit Yvette. Someone made me a faulty map, she later apologized, said she should've told me to take the second fork to the right, not to the left. Made a heck of a difference."

"And then you got lost," Bob said.

"I was out there all night. Got caught in one of those sudden storms Pete talked about. The heavens came down and the bayou swelled up. Pretty frightening."

"Couldn't you have tooted a horn or something and gotten help?"

"Just shows how much you understand about bayou country. Seemed to me that the channels changed direction before my eyes. I had no radio, no cell phone, no bullhorn."

"But someone found you. How did that happen?"

"I heard a boat but it disappeared. I must have passed out. I had a weird, confusing dream. Next thing I knew I heard someone say I was dead. I felt paralyzed, couldn't get the words out, they said I had no pulse and my lips were blue. I tried to speak but I couldn't."

"When did you recover your speech?"

"When they said they were taking me to the morgue."

"That would do it," Bob said.

"You don't want to know who rescued me?"

"Who?"

"Doc Winnipeg."

"What was he doing out in the bayou?"

"Said he came to visit with Pete's wife, Yvette. He was told by Meg, Pete's assistant, that I had gone out there earlier but hadn't returned. He decided to go find me."

"Good thinking," Bob said. "He may seem weird to us but he did find you."

"Oh, I'm more than grateful."

"You should be."

"It's somewhat strange to owe him my life. I'd rather it had been you. You would have called in the National Guard and mobilized a helicopter," I said.

"What he did turned out to be faster, I'm sure. But, speaking of the Doc, my accountant is looking at the financial statements for *Cliniques d'Haiti*."

"And?"

"Hardly any donors. Hardly any expenses. Hardly any cash flowing in and out. Looks like a small operation."

"Not what I would have expected," I said. "Was this just the past year?"

"Yes, looks as if they're shutting down."

"The lab on L Street left me a message at the hotel," I said.

"The vial," Bob said. "What did they find?"

"I wish I knew. A long Latin name."

"Call them back."

"Tomorrow. They're closed afternoons."

"It won't be drugs. Ricky doesn't use them," Bob said.

"But let's face it. How well do you really know him?

"I know him."

"Bet you haven't seen him more than a dozen times in that many years. And I know he's Gwen's father but that doesn't make him infallible."

"Okay, we'll wait and see tomorrow."

"I never saw Yvette," I said, "to tell her how sorry I am about Pete."

"Who found him?"

"His bus driver. A guy by the name of Orville. Not medically savvy by any means."

"Autopsy?"

"Not unless Yvette requests it, I imagine. And I don't know why she would."

"Let me see what I can find out," Bob said. "And another thing. I know you've been incommunicado for a couple of days but you need to listen to the weather forecast. It doesn't sound good."

"Fine," I said and turned on the TV.

It was true. Even if the eye of Hurricane Katrina passed to the east of New Orleans, they said, the wind from the north could force water from Lake Pontchartrain against the levees and enter the city. I'd heard it before but now it seemed like an irreversible fact.

I turned off the TV and called Topsy.

"What's going on," she said. "Can't get through on your cell phone. You have to charge it, you know. That's how they work."

"I've been out of circulation," I said.

"Doing what?"

"A long story."

"I have time," she said.

"Tell me about you, instead. What's new?"

"Okay. Martin Cook and I are going to the Kennedy Center tonight. He has season's tickets."

"See? I told you."

"He's cute but he's short."

"He's taller than you."

"I like to wear heels. Make my ankles look slimmer."

"You'll be sitting down at the Kennedy Center."

"Did you know Martin studied law?"

"No, I didn't, but doesn't everyone these days?"

"I don't want another lawyer. Jack was enough. I want an international banker, you know, like someone really smart from the World Bank or the IMF."

"Oh, like the one you set me up with, the one who absconded with millions from an African development project?"

"That was an aberration."

"Don't know about that."

"Or how about a staffer from the White House. Why not aim as high as I can?" Topsy was laughing now.

"Why don't you start with Martin and see how it goes?"

"Can't hurt."

After Topsy and I hung up I listened to the message from the lab several more times. At the end I had the Latin name down, more or less. Google supplied the rest of the explanation.

I immediately called Bob.

Chapter 59

I made a U-turn and pulled up behind the gray Chevy.

"Hey, you," I said and rapped on the window. I looked mousy in my wig and glasses.

He was slumped as usual and wore his dark shades. His face was black and shiny with perspiration. He rolled down the window and let out some stale air.

"You," I said. "Why don't you take the day off."

"What?" He smelled of beer and cigarettes.

"Tell Frank Smith I sent you home. Tell him I'll call and explain where I'm going today."

"Who's Frank Smith?"

"You know, the guy with the ski-jump nose."

"Who? And who the hell are you?" He'd seen me half a dozen times but never as Minnie Mouse.

I took out two of the four-inch nails and the hammer I'd bought at the hardware store. I went to his rear tire and drove the nails home.

"Oh, no," I said. "You'll have a flat in five seconds."

He was slow getting out. His belly was in the way. Too much beer. Too much junk food. Too little exercise.

I got to my car and slammed the door shut, started up, got myself in gear and took off before he even tumbled out on the sidewalk. I saw him in my rearview mirror watching the air ooze out of the tire.

The local radio station was still reporting on, as they described it, 'the Pete Brogan case.'

"It has come to our attention that a *Southwestern Oil* company executive is being questioned by the authorities," the announcer said. "Frank Smith, the company's director of public relations is answering questions about two deaths which have occurred on the oil rigs. A spokesperson for the oil company declined to comment. We understand a public statement will be forthcoming."

Frank Smith wouldn't have time to take phone calls and my fat friend in the gray Chevy would have his hands full for the next couple of hours. By the time they connected it would be too late. Frank might send someone else along but I'd worry about one problem at a time.

Cruising along past cemetery St. Louis #1 on North Rampart I spotted a man in front of the gate. It was Doc Winnipeg. I drove to the first corner, made a U-turn, came down on the other side and slowed down. Doc Winnipeg was hurrying back across the busy lanes.

After another U-turn I pulled up at the cemetery and got out of the car. A notice was tied to the wrought-iron gate. It said: *Attention. Cemetery temporarily closed. Oven vaults under repair. Dept. of Public Works*. The notice flapped in the wind and I re-tied the string like a good citizen.

Back in my car I cruised past Monique's house and around the block looking for a space. It came up six cars down at the left-hand curb where I could see the entrance to her house. I parallel parked in a tight spot on my first try. It's one of my many talents.

It was three-thirty in the afternoon and I settled in with a thermos of honest-to-goodness café-au-lait laced with chicory which I'd secured at the Café Du Monde. The three beignets were still hot and dripping with powdered sugar. They had given me an extra large handful of napkins.

The thing about a stake-out is it makes you sleepy. You sit around with nothing to do but keep your eyes peeled on a doorway. You can't read. You could talk on your cell but shouldn't. The coffee was supposed to keep me awake. It worked until about five-thirty when I must have dozed off. When I woke up it was seven and about to get dark. My wig had removed itself from the top of my head and had slid down over my eyes. This made it seem like the darkest of nights.

Half an hour later Monique walked out all dolled up for her first show at the *Blues Grotto*. She was in a long black dress with sequins and a feathered hat. Didn't look half bad tonight. She was alone and left in a red Ford. I struggled between my urge to eat some real food and my feelings of urgency about the case. I had just a few days left before my return to Washington on the 29th. I ate some stale potato chips and drank water. It didn't help a lot.

I sat in the car until, at nine, my endurance was rewarded. Antoinette walked right by me carrying a gym bag, crossed the street and knocked on Monique's door. Then she walked back to the curb and looked up and down the street. I slid down in my seat almost to the floor. When I re-surfaced Doc Winnipeg was locking the front door. Like Antoinette he stepped to the curb and looked up and down the street. I slumped some more.

They walked quickly to the corner and waited to cross North Rampart. The streets were very quiet. I got out of the car and shut the door with a gentle push and yet it clicked loudly. I stopped. They weren't talking. They stood at the side of the wide avenue waiting for cars to pass in the double lane. Then they walked quickly across to the grassy strip in the middle. The row of tall wrought iron lampposts—each with three opaque bulbs—were lit but spread no light to speak of.

They crossed the far lanes with Doc Winnipeg a few steps in front of Antoinette. She ran and caught up with him on the sidewalk They walked alongside the white-washed wall of St. Louis Cemetery #1 where the roofs of the tombs and the white statues of saints gleamed faintly.

There was one lonesome bush on the grassy strip next to a lamppost and I scooted across to the middle between cars. I crouched down behind the bush and waited.

They stopped at the gate to the cemetery. Doc Winnipeg searched in his pocket and came up with a huge key. The lock was rusty and squeaked like a cat in distress. The gate opened and he went in alone slamming it shut while Antoinette remained outside looking for all the world as if she had me in her sight. I flattened myself on the ground behind the bush.

The street was empty or I would have rushed back to the other side of the double lanes. Instead I was still there when Doc Winnipeg opened and shut the gate and walked across towards my puny bush with Antoinette.

I got up and ran like the devil. Never knew I could fly but that's how it felt. Now that I didn't need them, cars were coming up North Rampart in both lanes and I dodged between them, ran past Monique's house and reached my car.

My wig was askew and I'd lost the granny glasses.

I threw myself into the car, started up, and careened out of there just as Doc Winnipeg and Antoinette appeared in my rear-view mirror. They were walking slowly seemingly unaware of me.

I went around four blocks and called Bob.

Chapter 60

Bob answered my call on the first ring.

"We've talked to the authorities," he said.

"And they've confirmed?"

"Definitely."

"And the rest?"

"In place," Bob said. "Where are you?"

I looked out the window and saw a sign that said Dauphine.

"I'm on Dauphine," I said. "Parallel to North Rampart and three blocks from Monique's house."

"I thought you were supposed to watch the house. Seems difficult from a parallel street three blocks away."

"Things happened and I had to abandon my post. Temporarily."

"You've got to get back there," Bob said.

"I know. But Monique won't be home for at least another hour if I know her schedule. And I want Doc Winnipeg to settle down. He's such a nervous ninny. He'll ruin it all."

"What did he do?"

"Went to the cemetery with Antoinette."

"Hah."

"I followed them and crouched behind a pathetic bush. Doc opened the gate and went inside for about ten minutes. I couldn't move because he left Antoinette outside. When they crossed the street I had to run for it."

"Did they recognize you?"

"I'm hoping not. I was in my brown wig mode."

"Geez," Bob said.

"I'll give you a buzz as soon as something happens."

"I'm standing by," Bob said.

I took a detour a couple of more blocks away from Monique's house, found a small restaurant, walked out with a doggie bag fifteen minutes later—yet another Po'Boy sandwich—and a bottle of beer. Not that I like beer that much but they didn't have Hurricane cocktails in bottles. And I'm not having my innards eaten away by Coke.

I turned on the car radio and listened to the weather report. It was more than a weather report. It was Mayor Nagin calling for a voluntary evacuation of New Orleans saying he might order a mandatory evacuation by the morning. The National Weather Service had issued a bulletin predicting catastrophic damage to the city. They spelled it out. Partial destruction of half the houses. Windows blowing out in high-rise office buildings. Debris of trees, telephone poles, cars, and collapsed buildings. The city would be converted into a giant toxic marsh.

It was time to go. I called Topsy and left a message on her cell phone.

By eleven the Po'Boy sandwich was history and the beer, too, and I was feeling pretty good. I had the last of the Café Du Monde chicory coffee from the thermos and no dessert. Could have been worse.

At eleven-thirty Monique came home. The lights were on in the house and I saw Doc Winnipeg's shadow move back and forth.

At eleven-forty a car pulled up in front of the house and a woman stepped out from the driver's side. She went to the door, rang the bell, and returned to her car.

At eleven-forty-five Monique came out, walked across the street and got in next to the woman.

At eleven-forty-five-and-a-half they drove away.

At twelve-thirty Doc Winnipeg came out alone. He walked down the street. Not in a hurry. Just out for a walk.

I called Bob Makowski.

"We're on our way," I said.

I got out of the car in my brown wig and tried to look short. Doc Winnipeg took the same route as before. Across North Rampart. Waited on the grassy strip. Ambled across the double lane. A couple of cars were parked beyond the gate to the cemetery but otherwise not much traffic.

He took out his large key and opened the gate. He went inside. He slammed the gate shut and disappeared. I followed him across Rampart. The lock recognized my army knife and clicked open almost immediately. I jimmied it with a stone.

Just as I went inside the gate the gray Chevy pulled up and parked near the corner. No one got out but a dark form slumped in the driver's seat. The engine was turned off, the lights dimmed, and the interior went dark.

Chapter 61

St. Louis Cemetery #1, August 27, 2005

He had taken a right inside the gate.

I could hear the gravel crunching under his feet. I walked in step with him so he wouldn't notice the gravel crunching under mine. He stopped several times and I swayed to keep my balance. I looked around for a place to hide but the tombs on this side were too small.

I retreated towards the gate. I turned left and went down the now familiar path. When I got to the mausoleum with the black chain I stepped inside and got behind the tomb itself. I heard his heavy steps coming towards me.

He was pushing a large wheelbarrow.

I knew where he was headed and stayed where I was. Watching and waiting. He stopped in front of the last vault in the wall and I crouched down. Watching.

He had a crowbar in the wheelbarrow and inserted the sharp end into the bottom of the vault. He twisted the iron around and pulled. Nothing happened. He took out a hammer and began chipping away at the cement.

It took him half an hour to loosen the door. When he was almost done he sat down on the edge of the wheelbarrow and breathed heavily. He took out a bottle from his inner pocket and swilled something. His hair looked silvery in the faint light. He wiped his mouth with the back of his hand and got up.

The door to the vault was heavy and after he pried it loose from the last piece of cement the slab fell to the ground and broke into pieces. He stepped on top of the rubble, pulled out surgical gloves from his pocket, and put them on. Then a mask on his face. He reached inside the vault.

He pulled.

The stench was overpowering. It blew towards me. I struggled with the tickle in my throat.

He wrestled with an unwieldy form in gray sacking. He gave a last tuck and caught the bundle in his arms. He staggered with it to the wheelbarrow and dumped it in.

I sneezed.

He whirled around and tore off his surgical mask. I stepped out from hiding. He saw me.

He charged towards me in the dark.

He was faster than I'd imagined. And tall. Maybe an inch taller than me. His fists were clenched. He was going for a head butt. I let him come until he was an arm's length from me. I took a deep breath. I gripped his shoulders. I let out my best "kihap" shout to put extreme force into the strike. My left knee drove into his solar plexus. He groaned and collapsed.

I kept him on the ground with my foot on his chest but he was too winded to move. I waited until he tried to sit up. I helped him up on his feet, leaned him against the wall and held him there with my left arm.

Then I popped him one on the nose with my right.

"That's for Ricky," I said.

I popped him another. Harder.

"That's for Brad."

Then I put all my weight behind the last one and broke his nose.

"And that's for Pete Brogan," I said.

He slumped and slid down the wall holding his nose.

"The solar plexus was for me," I said. "Sphoeroides testudineus. Tetrodotoxin. Nerve toxins. Zombi drugs. Toussaint brought the powder across on one of his illegal trips. You left the vial at Ricky's house when you killed him. Was he alive when you buried him?"

Doc Winnipeg moaned. His nose kept bleeding.

"You poisoned me when you "rescued" me in the bayou. But you didn't give me enough of the toxic powder, did you. Maybe you didn't have enough. Or maybe what you had was too weak. Even so, I had all the signs. I was conscious but immobilized. I heard the voices but couldn't speak. Like a zombi. You would have had me buried alive. But I woke up. I was lucky. Ricky and Brad and Pete got the full dose."

The stench from the wheelbarrow was overpowering. I pulled Doc Winnipeg up from the ground, twisted his right arm behind his back and pushed him down the path towards the gate.

"Your money laundering scheme has been uncovered," I said to his back. "You used your aptly named non-profit organization as a cover. I don't know about your clients but they must be big to have gotten the attention of the FBI. Drug money?"

Doc Winnipeg grunted and I gave his arm another twist.

"Antoinette found out that Ricky was an FBI agent. You killed him at his house with toxin in a vial."

"You knew a vault was available in the cemetery. You faked the last name from a family still allowed to use the cemetery. You filled out the paperwork and submitted it to the authorities. We have a copy of the certificate. They didn't double check and they didn't suspect you'd lost your license to practice."

He grunted again.

"You doubled up Ricky's body, put him in a canvas bag and stuffed him in the wall.

I twisted his arm. His elbow snapped and he howled.

"You found out who Brad Sorensen was. That he stayed in the bayou at a deserted cabin. You waited for him down at Pete's dock. You followed him to the cabin and killed him. You overturned his boat and left him in the water. You came back and removed his car. You found Bob Makowski's note and knew we were getting close."

We got to the gate and I turned him around and pushed him up against the wall again.

"Pete Brogan was your friend," I said. "He rescued you after your pathetic activities in Ohio. Did he find out about the money-laundering? Did he find out about Ricky and Brad?"

Blood was running from his nose. It looked crooked and thoroughly broken. His right arm dangled awkwardly. His face was white and his hair silvery.

"Well, did he? Did he?" I heard myself shout the words into the dark night. "He confronted you, didn't he? You killed him."

Doc Winnipeg spoke for the first time. In a nasal twang.

"Bitch," he snarled. "*You* posted the sign about repairing the oven vaults. I knew they wouldn't be doing that. Bitch."

"I knew you might know that," I said. "But I also knew you couldn't take the chance that they would open yours."

His rage gave him strength. He broke free from my grip. He yanked an open *gris-gris* bag out of his pocket. He lunged at me with a head-butt. I grabbed at him and we tumbled to the ground. He rolled away, his eyes stared, his hair spun around his head like a crazy halo.

Before I could get up he stood above me looking triumphant. He held the *gris-gris* bag over my head. I got up on my knees and grabbed at it. The bag came out of his hand and the black powder spilled down my neck to my shoulders and covered my bare arms.

"You will die," he shouted. "The poison will kill you. It works fast. You have twenty minutes, then you'll be dead. No one can save you this time."

He sat down on the ground abruptly and held his broken arm. The *gris-gris* bag fell on the ground. He scrambled to pick it up but I got to it before him. It was still half full.

I threw the rest of the powder in his face. It hit his eyes and he howled in distress. I pulled him up by his shirtfront, leaned him against the side of the wall, and raised my hand. He rubbed his eyes with his fist in frantic movements. His face was contorted and he moaned as if he was already resigned to die. My own skin crawled and I felt it shrinking around my bones.

I didn't hear her coming until she was right next to me. Monique was still in her black sequined dress and she was wearing stage make-up. Her face looked like a clown's with its bright blue eye-shadow and scarlet lips. Her voice was low and full of venom.

"No one else is going to die," she said. "You fool, fool, fool."

Doc Winnipeg turned his head at the sound and tried to open his eyes.

"The *gris-gris* bag is not full of Zombi poison. It's full of ashes and dried lizard skin and dirt from my rose garden."

He got his left eye open.

"Double-cross," he whispered.

I shuddered and brushed ashes off my head, my shoulders and my arms. It no longer felt like poison. It felt like ashes and dried lizard skin and dirt from a rose garden.

"I buried the poison under my roses," Monique said. "I was never a part of these atrocities. It was Antoinette."

"I know," I said.

The three FBI agents burst through the gate waving their guns. They were blond with new crew cuts and clean-shaven faces. Looked like Ricky and Brad but not much like Don Levine. The FBI had mixed it up.

"What took you so long," I said.

"Just following orders, ma'am," one of them said.

"Orders from whom?"

"Makowski, ma'am. Said to give you satisfaction. He was yours to capture."

"He's yours now," I said and handed Doc Winnipeg over.

"Don't think he could have taken much more," the other one said. "Karate?"

"Tae Kwon Do. And plain old arm twisting."

"We watched," he said. "What did he have in the bag?"

"Ashes, dried lizard skin, and rose garden dirt," I said.

"Yes, ma'am."

"I'll explain later," I said.

"We're holding one Antoinette Bazile and one Toussaint Leautaud on accessory to murder."

A woman came in through the gate.

"This is my sister, Brandy," Monique said.

"I want to give a statement," Brandy said.

"We'll get it later," one agent said.

"Whores," Doc Winnipeg screamed.

"Do you know who's in the gray Chevy outside?" I said.

"That's one of Doc's goons," Monique said.

"I had him confused for a while," I said and sent a silent apology to Frank Smith although he didn't deserve it.

The three FBI guys had Doc Winnipeg in handcuffs. His nose was bleeding steadily and his right arm hung loose.

"Say goodbye," one of them said. "You're going away for a long time. Maybe forever."

"Bitch," Doc Winnipeg said and spat on the ground at my feet.

"Buh, bye," I said.

Hurricane Katrina—400 miles wide with waves 50 feet high—blitzed New Orleans on the morning of August 29, 2005. The category 4 storm passed through the area at 125 miles per hour, breaching the levees. Water surged in from Lake Pontchartrain and soon eighty percent of the city, including the French Quarter and the Ninth Ward, was flooded. Fifteen square miles of wetlands were destroyed. By the time the authorities ordered total evacuation it was too late. They had no rescue plan in place. Water levels in some places reached 14 feet and residents hacked their way up onto roofs, were rescued by helicopter, or swam or paddled their way to safety. But not all. The death toll was estimated to be more than 1800.

The last flight out of New Orleans left on August 28, 2005.

Epilogue

Bethesda, September 14, 2005

"Son of a gun," Bob said.

"You can say that again."

"Where is he now?"

"They got him to Baton Rouge before Katrina hit New Orleans. Awaiting trial. Three counts of murder, one attempted murder—that would be me—and money laundering," I said. "That's the trail Ricky Wilson and Brad Sorensen were following."

"Big case," Bob said. "Drug money has been going through hundreds of paper companies like *Cliniques d'Haiti* without a trace, to the Bahamas, the Caymans, to Switzerland. The records you stole from Antoinette's house helped. The FBI was in the last stages of unraveling the schemes when you and I stepped in and muddied the waters."

"They couldn't shake us loose," I said. "And they didn't know about the cemetery."

"Your poster from the Department of Public Works did the trick," Bob said. "Nice touch. And the guys behaved like gentlemen at the end. They let you get him."

"Antoinette and the Doc withdrew large amounts of cash from the bank in Port-au-Prince—helped by accomplices who lived high on the commissions—then made several stops on their way back to the States and deposited the money," I said.

"What happened to Antoinette and Toussaint?"

"They disappeared from the detention cell in New Orleans after the hurricane hit. Police guards were busy elsewhere. My guess is they're back in Haiti. They'll get caught eventually. Unless Don Levine pussyfoots around."

"What was Toussaint's role in all this?"

"He's a former Tonton Macoute. Had drug connections before Antoinette met Doc Winnipeg."

"How did the Doc get to the zombi poison?"

"The *gros Negre Voudou Houngan* I saw leaving Antoinette's house delivered it."

"What do you hear about Monique?" Bob said.

"Lost her house to the flooding and her jazz club to the creditors. She has returned to Ohio."

"And Brandy Gregory?"

"Brandy was safe in Baton Rouge when Katrina hit. She's still there, mourning Ricky Wilson."

"And Yvette?"

"Yvette has taken over Pete's ferry boat business. She'll bring a stern seriousness to the job if the tourists ever return."

"Did Margie Brown ever get her compensation from *Southwestern Oil* for her husband's death?"

"The autopsy showed her husband died of head injuries and not of a heart attack. She's suing *Southwestern.*"

"Good thing you made it back in time," Bob said. "The 28th was the very last minute."

"Caught the last flight, too," I said. "Thanks to Topsy."

"And Jon Douglas?"

"His house was flooded within half an hour of the 17th Street Canal levees breaking. He didn't get to use the hatchet. He pushed the canoe out the door, threw in his backpack and paddled away until the hole in the boat just under the waterline got bigger. The canoe filled with water and capsized within minutes. He was picked up by a good Samaritan and ended up at the Superdome."

"He was lucky."

"And resourceful. From the Superdome he made it to a UPS depot, hijacked a truck, picked up a family of four standing on the bridge, drove the truck to Baton Rouge, unloaded the family of four and left the truck at the local depot."

"He's back in Washington?"

"Yes, in time for his season at the jazz club in Georgetown. He's donating the proceeds from his first month to the Red Cross for Katrina flood victims."

"And now you're dating a thirty-something?" Bob said.

"Yes. Too bad you and Gwen split up," I said.

"Topsy is taking me in hand. Says she'll find me a woman in my own age group. How pathetic is that?"

"She's good at match-making."

"You're not bad yourself. She's dating Martin Cook."

"Yes, it's Martin here and Martin there. Turns out they have a lot in common. She's become a happy divorcee."

"I'm joining your next tour to Europe. There's gotta be more to life than crime." Bob said.

"Works for me."

www.ingramcontent.com/pod-product-compliance
Ingram Content Group UK Ltd.
Pitfield, Milton Keynes, MK11 3LW, UK
UKHW041848190726
13854UKWH00002B/777